T0032641

NIGHTS FROM THIS GALAXY

NIGHTS

SARABANDE BOOKS • LOUISVILLE, KY

THIS

Publisher's Cataloging-in-Publication Data

Names: Weitzel, Wil, 1967– author.
Title: Nights from this galaxy / Wil Weitzel.
Description: Louisville, KY : Sarabande Books, 2023
Identifiers: ISBN: 978-1-956046-06-9 (paperback) | 978-1-956046-07-6 (e-book)
Subjects: LCSH: Animals—Fiction. | Nature—Psychological aspects—Fiction.
Travelers—Fiction. | Human-animal relationships—Fiction. | Danger—Fiction.
LCGFT: Short stories. | Animal fiction.
Classification: LCC: PS3623.E46211 N54 2023 | DDC: 813/.6—dc23

Cover and interior design by Alban Fischer.
Printed in the United States of America.
This book is printed on acid-free paper.
Sarabande Books is a nonprofit literary organization.

This project is supported in part by an award from the National Endowment for the Arts. The Kentucky Arts Council, the state arts agency, supports Sarabande Books with state tax dollars and federal funding from the National Endowment for the Arts.

FROM

WIL WEITZEL

GALAXY

LION

When the old man died, I laid him out in the bathtub because he was small and neatly fit. I took him by the ankles first and then, moving slowly toward his neck, gently scrubbed him down. I lifted him at the back and washed his ribs all the way around until he was like an old moist cigarette. Then I dressed him the way he always dressed, in a corduroy suit—this one was a dun brown—and laid him in his bed and called his wife.

No one had been able to tell me why they lived apart. She was the one, most of them said, who insisted upon it. She needed relief from their intimacy, or she'd never loved him at all, or she was someone who thought only of herself. There were many reasons thrown about by the people who'd known the old man when he was young and teaching at the university or by others who cared for him now in his home as a paid occupation.

They were all women, these people of the house, who had keys and came in and out and bought food and delivered it and even ate some of it, standing in the narrow pantry and gazing at the shelves. Pickled artichokes and Sicilian olive oil and healthy breads from the best, the purest companies would come to rest in the cupboards. Often, I would eat with them, and they would talk of the old man in his presence as though he were only partially there.

He *was* only partially there. He was as old as old trees, their bark haggard or worn, that have survived the succession of the forest and long seasons of shade then the drought years of bone-dry springs and catastrophes of wind. He had long, tired memories that flowed in and out of events just like the wind. And up until the end, he had great gaps like any dry forest where he knew nothing at all about his life and it was as though it had never happened.

•

While I was attending my classes at the graduate school, he'd invited me through a colleague—as a favor to his former department and because I was an international student—to live with him. It was an honor to live with such a one. There were rumors of his teaching, of how he'd reached people, even the most remote, and left a mark on their lives. He had survived atrocities, it was said, while still a young man and was not supposed to be alive. To me, though, he appeared only a sad, old lord or a herald of brighter times which had faded until he had faded.

"More soup, I see," he would say over our soup in the low, dark living room that creaked like a boat with uneven boards at the floor and his books hovering above us as though they were preparing to fall from the walls. "More soup and more soup."

"It's wholesome soup," I'd tell him, encouragingly. "You should have more."

He would only grunt in such moments and reply, "So they say," then slurp his canned pea soup as if he were suddenly the ocean and it was a great turbulent river he was swallowing from the hills.

•

Once, during the last year I lived with the old man when my program of study was nearly complete and I was preparing to shove off again to points unknown, I told him the story of the lion, about a young boy in southern Africa who'd grown up on polished tile floors in a household of tutors and money with a lion cub. They had been forced to release the lion into the bush eventually, when he had become so powerful and strong that even the boy, who loved him, could not in good conscience hold him any longer inside the courtyard.

Years went by and the lion allegedly flourished at first under the eyes of authorities, until they lost track of him in the wild. They thought that perhaps he had migrated to the north where there were green, algal lakes and the herds slept in ancient gallery forests for longer segments of the year. No one knew exactly what had happened to the lion, but the prides had been shrinking for years in the scrublands and their prey had been gently seeping out of the blackthorn and crossing the burnt pans and fossil riverbeds to drift off into the hills. Finally, when for several brief seasons of rain there had been no word, the boy who was already a grown man and the pride of his family went out searching northward for the lion, carrying no weapon and against everyone's advice.

"By now," I explained quietly, staring up at the rickety shelves, "he's been gone a long time." I could feel my voice catch. "It's possible now that he will not go back."

I assured the old man that honestly I didn't know the rest of the story. We were sitting together drinking cognac, which I never drank but only smelled when I raised my glass to keep him company. He didn't much watch me anyway but only listened through his one good ear with a kind of ferocity when I spoke. It was in the winter when for weeks it had done nothing but snow until a layer of white had risen above the lower sills of our windows and I'd been shoveling for the old man so he could walk slowly from the house to the street through a high, narrow corridor constantly refilled. In those days, I awoke early in the mornings and went back to my shovel.

The old man stared at me directly, as he had never done before, when I told him there was no more to the story. Or that, if there was more, then I couldn't tell it. Because I wasn't yet sure how it ended. He glared at me from behind his heavy glasses with both eyes squinting intently, furiously it seemed, and waited a long time. He began to list in his chair as though we were poised together on a restless sea.

"Tell me this story again," he said finally.

"That's all I know," I told him.

"Again."

•

For months, all the way into May when the snows had melted at last and he drank *kir* rather than cognac and all I did around the house was empty the garbage, I told him the story of the lion. He in turn would tell me of Russia during the war and of the cold and how everyone had been hungry. He would come back to his hunger again and again as though it were the line that held him to the present, the long filament he followed backward into his life.

"What would you eat?" I'd ask. "What would there be for dinner?"

"For dinner"—and he'd pause, hovering over the bowl, then clean his spoon and place it carefully down on the table.

Sometimes for the rest of the meal, even after I'd heated more red lentil soup and come back to him hunched at the table, he'd say nothing. Then just when I'd think he was asleep in some inward way that was deeper than sleep and I was sneaking glances to measure the strength of his breathing, or just when it felt like I should turn on his Schubert or repeat a host of questions from which he could choose one, or that I should dim the lights nearly to nothing and silently step out of the room, he would ask me to tell him again about the lion.

•

On his last day, it was unseasonably cold and the women who came in and out to make his bed or gather his laundry or arrange the mail or deliver his Belgian chocolates must have been shuffling their schedules or preoccupied with others who were sick or elderly in other parts of town. His wife, as usual, was nowhere about.

When I returned from class the old man was bent at the table alone in the low, dark room that buckled beneath the world as though it had sunk to the very bottom.

I was silent. It was my final semester. I'd been living with the old man for nearly two years. I sat there with him and tried not to move at all.

"I've been remembering all of it," he said suddenly, loudly for one so close, as though he were a broad standing clock that had at last hit the hour. "It's all coming back."

"Tell me," I urged him.

"First, I should think," he said very slowly, the way he said all things, with great spaces of silence stretching in between, "you should speak again about the lion."

I drew out the childhood of the boy in great detail, lingering over the way the sun smote the tiles of the courtyard, the way the lion would turn over onto his back in the afternoons in the shade of the mopane tree, and how if one stepped beyond the walls one needed to watch for the long, curved sickles of acacia thorns. For as long as I could do it honestly, I deferred the ending. Finally I came to the part about the boy, grown up, leaving the great sprawling farmhouse in the south and climbing the first escarpment, gazing back down at the maize fields belonging to his family. I related yet again that with twin weights of sadness and longing in his heart, he turned to wander out toward the lion.

Throughout these moments the old man ticked soundlessly beside me, swaying slightly in his chair, nodding now and again with a calm I would never have believed in, as if to encourage me. I admitted then for the first time what I hadn't told a soul, that the boy's father had assured him if he left on such a fool's errand—which he, the father, could explain to no one—if he threw himself at the world without so much as a knife at his belt, and if, of all things, he sought a lion that outsized him four and a half to one, then he was not welcome to return. It would be a final parting. He had no place in their lives.

And I could tell as I went on, stumbling at first then gaining my courage, the old man had been patiently waiting for my story through the length of our long winter, and after so many years of searching and for the second time in my life I was suddenly alone.

COYOTE

I got as far as Boise, Idaho, which is pretty far, when I knew I was going the wrong way. There was no official money to help departing staff back at the predator rescue center in Nebraska, but the two biologists insisted on giving me bus fare. If things had been different, I wouldn't have taken it. I like to believe that. But I did take it because I wanted to get west to the ocean.

In Boise, there's a cheap place for meals I knew about from when I was working for the municipals doing bridge repair south of Idaho Falls and moonlighting as a courier, mostly for the ski company, Sun Valley. I never got close to the resort—stuck in cities—but I met this woman who covered the morning shift at the café, starting at six thirty. For a long time, maybe a month and a half, I was her first customer.

"Here to help me open?" she used to joke when she'd find me out shuffling in the cold. I would haul up their blinds and bring the chairs down from tabletops. She'd serve me black coffee, first of the day, then before the old-timers came in she'd sit down at the table and cross her legs.

I never touched her. Even so, there was that tension, coming from the possibility I'd invite her out somewhere, or reach across and fold my hand over hers. Or ask if she liked floating rivers still coursing through their beds far to the north and could get a week off. I'm not sure she would have been altogether against any of that.

But I took it mainly as kindness on her part. Maybe loneliness. Still, you see her face. It blends in with the hot feel of the coffee. The smell of the place in the morning before anything's been spilled.

Now, when I got off the bus in Boise, well short of Oregon, which was where I thought I was headed, I made it over to this café. I figured I'd spend a night in town then get back on the road. It was three years since I'd been in Boise. But everything looked the same. Inside the place, there was no waitress because it was past the dinner rush. And I didn't expect to see her anyway. I think I was a little afraid to find her working there after that amount of time. I believe if I'd spied her coming from the kitchen with that same hand-sized spiral notepad, it would have made me want to bus tables and walk around with a clean shirt taking orders and delivering tabs, so she could go out and look for something else.

Anyway, there was the same old, spindly cook I'd met a few times before. He didn't own the place, but he used to come in around ten o'clock and we would exchange a few words, on the rare occasions I was hanging around at that hour. He'd start prepping for the lunch crowd and make a hell of a lot of noise back in his small kitchen. Walter, his name was. I remembered that.

"I've got something for you, Walt," I told him now, fresh off the bus. I knew he'd watched me in the old days with that waitress. The familiar looks, I guess, she and I would send back and forth. Though, despite the tired way she'd shrug and laugh, then kick softly at a chair leg when I said just about anything, the two of us knew next to nothing about one another.

The cook, Walter, looked a hundred years older. He stared at me now when I leaned over the counter.

"You got some time later on?" I asked.

I could tell he was surprised. I didn't look good. I got pretty battered the night they attacked that rescue center. My arm was in a sling. I had a long, deep gash running under my eye that stung when I opened my mouth. But I was right about him. The idea to look him up came when my confusion hit its peak. Sitting on the bus, I thought of that serious-minded old cook before we'd even crossed out of Wyoming, when state signs for Moose and Hoback sent me memories of Grand Targhee and the deep snow in those mountains and their steep ravines and a whole era of my life. I'd expected him to be at the café. Though the waitress was sure to be long gone, settled in some neat house in another state, he wasn't the kind to change jobs. His sad, exhausted eyes set over cheeks caved just enough to leave questions about his teeth left a stark picture in my mind.

Now the tight features relaxed, started to separate. The eyes took on that little bit of water. His tiny, raw-boned frame heaved out its bass voice, ballooning from the depths of him.

"All right then," he said. "When we close if there's something you need to talk out."

I gave Walter the full scoop. I hadn't opened up to anybody in years. And it's only a type of openness. But tell a stranger a thing you've never worked through, his face right there can let you know which parts are the ones that matter and where you're just circling around.

"I haven't been out in the woods since I was young," said Walter, feeling his way. "So I couldn't say. Myself. But if I had to—"

He stood up after an hour and a half because it had grown emotional between us. I laid it on him, everything that happened, my wandering, the seasons in the backcountry, for nearly twenty years. Then events at the predator rescue center. The night of the raid, which haunted, left its cold print on me.

"I haven't heard this one before," said Walter. "Not exactly. So I can't truly advise you. But if I had to advise you—and I do see you're pushing me—" He looked over warily, as if I'd turned into his mortal enemy. He looked particularly at my shoulder pulled back so the clavicle would set, as if that's where my heart, or the thing he was talking to, was specifically located.

"No, I haven't been out there to those relict forests. Mostly been right here in Boise. Though I have spent time on the river back when it was flowing more regularly—" He cut himself off and shook his head like he was deeply disgusted at the mention of his own life circumstances.

"But I can see all the way out there to what's left of the wild spaces. I got line of sight—not on your rusted pine. Not those bottomland wastes of larch and alder—not snags and burnt timber. I mean the last fir belts still growing up sides of mountains. Black spruce that's stunted, sure, hurt by pestilence, our toxic winds, but remain alive in high country. I know what those trees look like when it's first getting dark, even if I can't see them anymore. Their leeward bottoms grow that much thicker for starts—such is the feeling they'll give you."

I nodded fiercely to encourage him because I could sense Walter was getting close to it, whatever it was. He looked riled, taken by fever.

"And that stays with you, let me tell you. You don't need to travel out to those areas making their last stand. You'll know them by instinct—now. That's your one word for it."

By this point, Walter was walking around the café like it was his house. I was sitting, huddled and small, trying to make myself smaller, more insignificant, at a center table he'd chosen. Meantime, he was on the move. Touching walls. Changing the hang of the old photographs of warehouses and cattle barns. Performing invisible adjustments on the napkins, each a quarter turned from the one below, piled up to make a neat, alternating star.

"In your blood, now, right? No other word. I don't have to go out there again in my life to know."

I gave Walter every indication I was knowing too. I opened my eyes wide and closed them and brought my shoulders up and down, a little painfully, to emphasize my breathing.

"I can hear them go quiet—they're pockets of life. Where you've still got the denning animals. They're sheltered by something. Rocks maybe. Or trees. The cut banks of rivers. What's that going to mean," Walter asked, "when we lose those last refuges—and not just us?"

I was afraid to break the spell. I realized the café was a little like those forest places he was describing. A holdout. Maybe a sanctuary. Walter was winding down. He was skeletal, an old white guy who'd lived in Boise his whole life. I'd laid out my years drifting back and forth, sleeping where there were woods, or in somebody's guest room, a garage. Trekking through drifts sometimes far off from people. And he'd just spent himself savagely in those forests he knew only from imagining them.

"Never once heard someone explain it that true," I told him.

Walter sank back to the table and collapsed on his chair, and we were two slumped figures. I could see us from a long way above. As though that café where the waitress used to work had no roof on it anymore. I was looking down on Walter, who was a gray-and-white speck, and this other broken form that must have been me, slung up in a collarbone harness.

"You say he put his back to you then?"

"That's right."

Walter's deep voice got real quiet, confidential, as he finally closed in on the center of his concerns. Like finally they were rising from the earth toward us both.

"And he hurt them, you say. Did some damage to those men."

"He did damage."

I went through it again, more slowly this time, with all the details I could remember. How I'd worked as a janitor, at first, hosing down pens at the predator rescue center in Nebraska. When there was political trouble surrounding the center, I took shifts as their security guard. First thing, a pair of local men with livestock interests came to threaten the two biologists, a young man and a woman, who were there for the winter on an internship. Meantime, the two lead scientists, married with a child, were on leave for those coldest months, and the caretaker of the facility was a retired grocer who didn't live on-site.

"We're going to shut this whole thing down," said one of the guys who showed up. "Best thing now is just you head back right where you came from."

"Don't try to protect these killers," the other one chimed in, pointing over toward the feeding area. "Or make excuses. They kill. That's what they do." This second man, who was short and squat, made a grotesque expression, squinting and contorting his mouth. "Pre-da-tor," he said slowly, sounding out the word on the sign outside the facility, for the benefit of the biologists. "But now see—" The man made a line in the dirt in front of him with the stiff heel of his boot, then deepened it. "That would just mean killer."

"These animals are innocent," I said, stepping up beside the biologists. They were fidgety men standing in front of us, and I was pretty sure they'd been put up to this. "We ate most of their range away, or it's dying back, piece by piece. So coming after your penned goats and chickens is what they've got left. Their world's going away."

"That's a sad story, mister. Now look, see, you've got the tears coming. Why don't you be sure to be here then—when we come back."

I looked over at the faces of the biologists. They were directed at me in anticipation. I'd never said much before. Just taken the job scrubbing tiles because I needed some way to feed myself. Quietly, they began backing toward their cramped office.

"You got a specific time?" I asked the men once the biologists had made it to their office. "Because I'm a planner."

One of the two laughed loudly, but the other, the squat one, didn't laugh. He stared at me hard.

"Good to know, mister. Now see"—he wrinkled his nose like he'd caught the sudden scent of an animal hidden just behind or somewhere inside me—"I'm real glad you let that out."

I suggested the biologists, who'd alerted the police, stay nights at the Days Inn in town. The rescue center was past the outskirts, far in the northern section of the state. Surrounding tall grasslands were hit hard by desertification, but part of a prairie recovery project that, if funding came through, was to become a reserve. A local rye whiskey manufacturer had put a wolf on its bottle to garner funds for the project, and the area was just large enough to serve as a trial reintroduction zone for displaced animals, including those from the refuge. It was still fenced, but big enough to allow the animals to hunt in the scablands, along a fossil river, and into degraded ash and yellow beech stands. But that hope brought bitter resentments and much debate in the local gazette. The animals, meanwhile—a juvenile cougar, pair of female gray wolves, five bedraggled prairie coyote pups, and one large, restless, shaggy, and displaced eastern mountain coyote—looked like they were in slow-brewed shock, maybe unaware of what swirled around their heads, but surely conscious of captivity, of walls.

I explained to Walter in that café how by the night the men came back I'd had the dark shift for two weeks. How I carried no weapon because I'd assured the biologists the men would be armed and my own weapon was bound to bring fire. It would encourage them to shoot animals. The biologists had shaken their heads at this logic, but I'd insisted. Local police officers visited and swore to include the facility on patrol routes, but they couldn't dedicate a squad car. One thing for sure, when the moon rose over those struggling edge lands, the animals and I were out there all alone.

There were five of them, more than I'd figured. I told Walter how I came down on the first one who had a rifle from the low roof of the coyote building where I'd stowed all the animals. How one man worked the door while the others laid into me. How, when one got me in the low shoulder with the crowbar, that side of my body went hard and cold. Without any power.

I explained how once we were inside the squat, bunker-like building they went for the coyote pen first. How the ceiling was low and they were wearing headlamps, so lights flared out in all directions and crashed under the dim, flickering fluorescents. How the prairie pups cowered together in a mass in the back of the pen.

And how the big one, the mountain coyote, stayed in the rear and sheltered them with his body.

Then when I told him how one of them pulled his handgun and ducked into the pen, Walter stood up abruptly from the table and started pacing again.

"They'd hurt my left shoulder, but my right was still strong."

"Good," said Walter. "That's good." He looked toward his kitchen with great intensity. "Least we got that."

"One was down from my wrench outside the building, so there were just the four inside."

"All right, that's fine," Walter murmured. "Just four of them now."

The big mountain coyote growled but didn't move when the man raised his pistol and said something I don't remember. "Here's this" or "You're done." Something like that. But just then I took hold of his arm and there was somebody on my back in that same second, and we fell all scrambled into the large pen.

"I got up first," I told Walter.

"Course you did," whispered Walter, staring now, I could see, at his knives, which were hung neatly, according to size, on a long magnetic strip that ran above the low shelving. They looked too perfect to cut something. Too clean from my angle. Like they were museum pieces.

"I got over the gunman. Broke his wrist because I could hear it on the cement floor of the pen. But the other man cut me with a short knife I hadn't seen. He swung it in big motions rather than use it with knowledge, and once it came over across my face."

"Goddamn him," said Walter. "But that one now—" He straightened up his body at the thought, seeming to jump forward in the story, having heard it already. He started toward the open kitchen, moving slowly. His hands came out from his hips. I could tell he was choosing his weapon after long years of knowing exactly what does what and how well.

"That man did get caught in the throat," I finished for Walter. "That was when the big mountain coyote lunged from the back of his pen."

Walter glided past his culinary knife row like those knives were bright phantoms, unusable. He bent down toward a low drawer I couldn't see, beneath the level of the counter. Then he rose up with a dark, single-barrel shotgun. It was heavy, I could tell. It weighed on his thin-set shoulders and rickety frame. The stock was of an old, fine wood, wire filigreed, and the action had been polished to shine under the lamps of the café.

"Those two men were both down then," I went on. "Not moving. I couldn't see their weapons straight off."

"So you stepped out of that pen," said Walter without looking at me.

"I'd been cut at my ribs but didn't know it yet. There was the wound on my face pouring in my mouth. Two of us, we came out, him behind me."

"You and the animal," Walter confirmed, sighting something now on the far wall. There was a painting there. Some cheap-framed hillscape draped with lush, green primary forest that dated from an earlier era, maybe Walter's era, and looked now dense and impossible.

"They spread out, those two men still up, at the perimeter of the room. He was snarling terribly at my back. Then both the men came in, both with something hard, maybe a pipe, crowbar."

"That's all right," pronounced Walter with great concentration. "We got ourselves even numbers now." He was sighting something in the old forest at the far end of the room. It must have been large by the look of him. Something, I presumed, he couldn't miss. His arm, the shoulder, were absolute, unwavering.

"Only one of them made it as far as me. And my wrench was lost back in the pen. I took a beating. But the fight behind me was real short. It probably wouldn't be called a fight."

I could see Walter was waiting patiently for me to go on and retell that last part. He was poised now for his shot. He didn't have a scope, but he was contorting his wrinkled face to squint down the long, thin, polished barrel.

"The man back behind me yelled hard. Then just small stuff, soft curses, barely talking."

Walter pulled the trigger. The chamber was empty, but I could hear the bolt snap back, and the dry sound of the action stayed in the air afterward. He lowered his gun, a great weariness come over his face.

"When my guy stumbled out of the building," I went on, "the coyote stayed over the man down beneath him and sniffed his hair, one ear, then his neck, and wavered a few seconds. Then he limped back into the big pen and stood over the others. When nothing was coming, no more fight, he sank back to those prairie pups."

Walter was quiet for a long time, taking everything in. "That's good. Then that's fine," he said at last. "Now I'm real sorry to do this to you."

"You don't have cartridges, Walt."

"I don't need those."

"All right."

He had the gun pointed toward my heart.

"That girl you knew here—well, you know she's dead."

I realized I'd underestimated Walter badly. Turns out he had an elephant memory. Thinking too I was just one in the droves that came through.

"She's killed by a mugger. In these streets. Waiting for her boyfriend ten blocks from right here where you're sitting. In winter." Walter coughed up something that sounded bigger than he was. "January at that time. She was going home from work here."

"All right."

He walked toward me, as if his gun held shot pellets he could spray into my chest and then, for effect, over my side of the room.

"I'm sorry," I said.

"No, I'm sorry."

He brought the gun barrel up to my chest and printed the bead sight on me firmly, just below the slanting crosscut of my shoulder harness.

"Now, I don't need cartridges for what I'm going to say."

Walter looked in that moment like he was barely alive. He was old and tired as could be. The pressure on my chest stayed steady though, important.

"You got my attention."

"Now he's calling out to you, that animal, over the miles you've gone away."

"Calling out."

"That's what I just said."

Walter brought the gun back from my chest and turned it around slowly, like the arm of a clock. When it was vertical, he pressed the whole thing the long way into my good arm.

"Take it," he said hoarsely. "Don't you leave him there like that unprotected. Our whole world's coming now for its last animals."

"They've got police, Walt."

Walter had come over to my good shoulder and was trying to hoist me out of my chair.

"I don't care who you think they've got. Police won't work. Not what he's up against. You're connected now." He spoke that word with terrific meaning and looked me straight in the eye to be sure it got through. He shook his arms violently toward the sky and flung his hands down at the ground so I thought they might just strip off him.

"All there is to it. You gotta turn yourself around."

When I walked into the rain in Boise it was after another hour and we'd made settled agreements about where I needed to go and it was deep night and Walter was there in the lit-up doorway of the café, nodding at me, shooing me away, and I was carrying an antique shotgun that belonged to an older West, too powerful, warmed by his hands, to be loaded to fire.

•

By the time I got back to the predator rescue center in Nebraska, the biologists were no longer there. They'd been making arrangements to move the animals before I left, and the pair of gray wolves and the young cougar were already gone. The caretaker was on-site during business hours and there were a part-time intern and several local volunteers who came in and out. But the couple who had founded the refuge were still out of the country. For the three days I was gone, a policeman supposedly had been true to his word and parked his squad car outside the building that held the remaining animals—all coyotes—for the lengths of the nights.

When I walked into the squat bunker, I saw they had him all on his own, as we did before the men first came to threaten the facility. He was half sleeping, the way he always slept, lids open just enough to give a view straight ahead. I walked over to his pen and crouched down beside the wide grate. The eyes shifted under his lids so I could see them do it. Then he rose, stiff at the left hip, forepaw wounded on that side from where he'd been struck by the raiders, and limped to the back of the pen. I wondered if they'd fractured his pelvic bone.

"Sure glad you're alive," I said.

He stayed standing in the rear, his body gone leaner, less muscular in those three days. I was filled with a rush of shame for leaving him, and sweaty relief at the same time.

"We must have hurt them worse than we thought."

That night, we moved him and the pups by truck into town, to the hospital precincts. They put him out, and veterinarians drove in and ministered to his hip. The founding couple, who were in Rwanda working with primates, arranged the whole thing. The biologists and I had spoken with them on the phone the morning after the raid, and the couple had hired lawyers. The police had interviewed me at length in my sad state. They'd asked for descriptions, had me sign forms. When I explained I'd hauled the three men who were left, one at a time, out to their truck with my good arm and shoulder, then stanched my rib wound with a sheet from the office cot, they'd looked at me hard. But I'd told them I didn't want those men, even in such bad shape, any nearer the animals than they had to be.

Now, since the biologists were gone, I stayed with him through almost all of it. He kept his eyes on my legs below the knees when I moved. After two days in a pod on the hospital grounds, a truck rolled in to transport him and the pups to another refuge outside

Asheville, North Carolina, and I offered to ride in the cab with the driver. The couple in Rwanda thanked me on the phone. They were tearful, I could tell, from their voices. The most generous kind of people. They kept saying, "Normally we'd have somebody there. You don't need to do this. If you've got to get out west directly—"

"I want to do this," I told them. "After what we've been through."

I didn't go so far as to say I was pretty sure he'd saved my life. There's no telling what those men would have done if they'd gotten the chance to unleash. To beat on me without holds. I believe they meant to shoot up the animals, then truck me out, hurting, somewhere. But I was afraid if I told anyone besides Walter about what he'd done they could put him down, so I framed the story to the police, even to the couple, as his rising up to defend those pups.

"Well, if you weren't there"—the man stumbled on the phone from Rwanda. "We sure do hate to think."

"It was two of us," I said. "Really was together."

As we ate the miles from Nebraska down into Missouri, I started spending some of them lying back in the trailer near the crates. I'd say things to him like "Just above Jefferson City now" or "Tell by the slowdown—that's St. Louis. Hang in there, though. We'll be through." He'd stare off toward the pups clumped up in another crate, their bodies crammed into a tight mass just visible between close slats.

In Evansville, Indiana, I bought a three-dollar beanbag at a thrift store and plunked it in the trailer and started singing to him, both of us coming in and out of sleep. I sang songs I'd heard from my mother—"Puff, the Magic Dragon" and "Mr. Bojangles"—and he brought his lids down almost to close. In Bowling Green, the driver and I got drunk in one of the smallest bars I've seen, with seats enough for seven people strung in a line together. I think the intimacy of the place, with the bartender leaning in so his thick whiskey breath swam over our ears, got us to drinking in earnest. Then, in London, Kentucky, I took the wheel for a while, which the driver explained was against all regulations. When I reassured him that I didn't have a license, so there were bigger problems that would prevent it from coming back to his job, somehow he took to that logic and we cranked the radio way up, and then, when that ran dry, moved to the proud stack of Grateful Dead bootlegs he kept under his seat.

The whole time, though, my mind was on something else. The driver, Mel, wore wide-frame, knockoff Ray-Ban sunglasses even at night, saying something about the contrast, and he was round as he was tall with a great head of hair flowing halfway down his back. He tilted that head back and guffawed at almost any story as if it were the most outlandish thing he'd heard. We traded the wheel back and forth beyond Knoxville, and I even convinced him to take a shift on the beanbag to keep the coyotes company. But mostly, as time wore on, Mel stayed up in the cab while I drove and shook his head at what seemed like the sadness of the world poured over by long, rising screeds of Jerry Garcia's guitar. "Damn shame," he said as the miles sank under us, and I could tell he'd gotten sentimental at the thought of our arriving at the predator shelter near Asheville and the prospect of the whole party ending.

We were in the mountains by then and I was starting to long to be away from the noise for a while. It was deep summer already, late June, and the deciduous trees that had hung in there at midelevation bore the heartbreaking green of full season. I was thinking a lot about Walter. But locked onto my mind with a vice grip through that whole trip was the shaggy, brindled, wide-ruffed, tawny-eyed eastern mountain coyote in the back. He looked shrunken and shapeless stuck inside his crate, an animal in deep mental and physical retreat. That's why I couldn't concentrate fully on the music. What I was thinking of was something like what I believe Mel began dwelling on in the broken forests that rose into the Smokies. I was thinking, little as it had felt like it in St. Louis, the trip was going to close out. We were going to pull that rig over and turn off its engine and they were going to unload those crates out from the back of my life.

•

The facility outside Asheville was much larger than the one in Nebraska, with many more animals. The couple in Rwanda had sent an email and notified the management I was looking for a job. The man who ran the place was kind and understanding, but he didn't have funding for additional positions. He seemed to have an intuitive understanding of my state, however, and said he'd let me feed the coyotes we'd brought along for a few days. They were kept in a separate building that was like an intermediary zone, before they would be relocated to one of the large, semicovered outdoor pens. It was stuffy in there, close quarters, with more of that same yellowish ceiling light they'd had at the other refuge.

Mel had four days off after his run from Nebraska, and he spent the first two days in town so we could rifle through the bars in Asheville for local, mountain-brewed beer. But the magic between us had worn down now we weren't moving. And I didn't feel like getting drunk.. So we said goodbye overformally, as though we were business colleagues who'd finalized the deal on a cargo shipment that was to come in far away, on another continent. I stood two blocks off the main drag in Asheville where he'd parked his rig and told him he shouldn't drive straight from the brewhouse.

"You of all people," he laughed, a little offended.

"Oh, I know."

I waved at his rearview, seeing him in there, hunched in that dark cab, for a few long seconds, before he hit second gear and started powering, loud and slow, out toward the interstate.

When I got back to the refuge, I found the small building with the coyotes locked up and retired to the bunk they'd set up in a side office apparently little used. That next morning, I asked if I could spend some time with the animals before I shoved off. I figured I could have invented some use for myself there. I could have gone back to fence repair and security shifts. I'd volunteered to catch on at a job before. But it was too sad. The place was businesslike. Well staffed. Everything was organized, properly funded, and in its place.

The manager, Ralph, had taken a liking to me. We had some sort of kinship based, I believe, on my wrecked beanbag, which he'd seen in the trailer bed beside the coyote crates and I'd moved into the holdover building. He slowed down when he talked to me and his eyes traveled out over my slung-up shoulder to show he was reflecting.

"I can't let you stay with them too long. You may already have done that," he said. "Because our focus here's still reintroduction." His boots were fidgeting a little on the asphalt and making a grating noise. "Less he sees one person, a human, gets comfortable, starts to trust, the better. Especially with his species." He looked up at the sky as if the fault were above us. "They're not so popular."

"We knew that out in Nebraska," I said. "Makes sense. But what he's been through. I don't think he's partial, if you've seen his paw, that hip, to humans."

Ralph laughed.

"Go on in there," he said. "Take your time."

But I wasn't long. We were already habituated. So it wasn't that. It was just I could sense the preview of the bad feeling I was getting, and half of me was hoping one of us would start hurting physically enough that I couldn't leave. Like maybe his hip would flare up in a way we'd have to deal with immediately. Or maybe my rib wound, which had been sutured, would start seeping dangerously.

"You'll be fine," I told him. "They'll let you out of here."

He looked over at the pups like he did whenever I spoke to him. In fact, whenever I walked into a building where he was penned, he'd wait to recognize me then immediately glance away. The only times I saw him stare at me in Nebraska were when I was coming or going, and then it was at my legs. Sometimes, when I turned back for something I wanted to check on, walking out from the bunker there, he already would have shifted his wide head and be deep-watching my movements under those weak, flickering lights.

"Ralph's a good man," I went on, but I was running dry. My ribs, my face wound were hurting. Stinging at the look of him. Just being there, inside another facility, without those tall wheels of Mel's rig to ride up on, brought back the hard touch of metal and knives.

"You take care," I told him. And then, though it hadn't been exactly in my mouth to say, "I won't be far off."

•

I said goodbye and Ralph played gruff, but I thought he was going to break down right there. I realized Mel must have worked on him after the unloading when I was inside the building with the animals. Mel, adjusting and readjusting his fake shades, could talk a blue streak. He must have told him about my hours on the trailer bed back with the coyotes. The five months I'd spent with those animals in Nebraska. Since Mel was the sensitive type, he probably relayed how I'd get quiet about the coyotes. Avoid questions about a bond or felt connection.

"You got a name for that coyote of yours?" Ralph asked me.

"No. Nothing like that."

"Big fella, though. Powerful through the haunch."

When Ralph was getting nowhere, he bid me farewell.

"You gonna haul that beanbag with you?" he asked after he'd given me a bear hug. Ralph was tall with a round potbelly and thin, knobby arms but he could deliver a hearty embrace. He looked at the contoured straps of the beat-up, high-volume backpack I'd angled over my good shoulder. He couldn't see the bandage I wore over my ribs or the heavy wrap I'd wound about my torso, but he could see my cut face and the grungy clavicle harness.

"You gonna be all right there?"

"High summer," I said. "Be just fine."

"Come to think of it—you know—we'll be moving them next couple days. Soon as tomorrow maybe. Sure you don't want to stick around least for that?" Ralph pointed over toward the holdover building. "'Fore you just rush off?"

I could tell he was offering me a job, and as I walked away, I thought I was making a big mistake, but I couldn't stop. How long can you scrub floors or mix ground meat and cornmeal or watch over quiet nights at a place while the world closes in on everything wild? I figured they'd get him to a larger enclosure where he could rely on predation, then reestablish him next door in the Smokies, if not way up in Algonquin. But now it wouldn't be until after another winter, into late spring when prey was more active and less concentrated. I knew from Nebraska wherever forest and prairie lands were drying out and fragmented, with habitats losing ground, intraspecies violence could kill released animals straight out of the gate.

I started walking down the asphalt drive. Then, when I thought I was clear of view around a bend, I jumped a wood fence and headed out into a grove of pitch pine. It was warm and bright and ten o'clock in the morning. Everything, in that slow breeze, was lit up and trembling. I needed to check in at the clinic to get my stitches removed, and so I took a shortcut through fallow sorghum fields and wound up in town two hours later on a direct route.

They fixed me up at the expense of the couple in Rwanda, who, working through Ralph, had given me the name of the clinic. At that point, I figured I'd follow the track Mel had cut toward the interstate. But my steps went instead from the clinic to the bar, and now I did get drunk on something they called Burial Beer. I wished to hell Mel hadn't deserted me and that I wasn't carrying Walter's old shotgun wrapped in a quarter blanket and toed down in my backcountry pack so I had to leave a bivvy sac draped loosely over the whole thing to disguise the front bead sticking out.

Then I wandered back the two hours to the woods outside the refuge and made camp. I ate a bag of pine nuts Mel had bought in central Missouri and opened a can of cannellini beans Walter had slid into a stash pocket of my pack. My ribs were sore as hell. I lay on my back watching the few stars revolve and was awake the whole night, so far as I could tell, looking at the same ragged patch of darkness between two twisted pitch pine limbs, resprouted from fire and making a wild second tree out of the ruins of the first, its thick, plated bark holding just the slightest light.

In the morning, I tried to pull myself together and was ashamed when what I wanted was to go back to the holdover building and loiter around the place and see what I could do to be of service. I made the sorry deal with myself I would check to see if they'd moved him already. I was thinking it might give me a picture, before I headed off, to see him just once in their more spacious semioutdoor pen. Tracing the perimeter fence, I figured. Scoping his boundary.

But Ralph caught sight of me from a long way off. It was just the luck of things, I guess, but I came up the road and was planning to stand inside the tree line and scan the large pens. I stared at him as he came out from the office, thinking it was early to be at work. He stopped in his tracks on the second step and stared right back like I was a ghost. I waved a little too long and when there was no response brought my hand down.

We stood there, the two of us, and I looked out over the pens and saw three slim subadult red wolves, gathered together far in the distance inside the outermost enclosure. But there were no other animals. I didn't have the heart to look any more at Ralph. I turned away from him and stooped low to hitch my pack a little higher and started away from the refuge down the asphalt road. I climbed back over the fence and checked my camp to make sure I'd left nothing. I evened out the ground where it had been damp under my weight, as I always did. It was the oldest instinct.

Then I set off through that same overgrown sorghum field and got an hour out, little more, when there was a dark, animal shape off my bow, right at the woods line, coming even with me, and my heart skipped a beat. I knew old Ralph had done it. It was so early, I guess he was the only one around. He'd opened the gate and made a test of it. And when that shape stayed even, I caught him now and then in my peripherals, not daring to look full-on, thinking, once I'd given it half an hour and we were dangerously near town, Walter was somewhere far out there at twelve o'clock, clattering his pans. And at the thought of him, still believing in the world, I turned my forty-five degrees and the coyote and I shaded together into the mountains, toward what forests were left.

RUN

Vincent lay in a makeshift bed he'd made in the dirt just shy of a line of lean-tos and a rickety outhouse that was raised up on stilts like a deer blind and commanded a view, in late fall, of the wash coming out of the hills and muddying the slopes toward the river. It was not a hiding place exactly, as the captain knew where it was. Then again, anybody on those acres could see him if they trained their eyes because he wore yellow, the electric yellow of a timberline safety vest that was far too large and stood on him like the hulking camo jacket of a junkie.

Vincent was always tired, so he spent time when he had it on his back. He had a leash secured to his belt, the large-buckled leather variety of belt with the brown buckle ground down by age and weather and dinged all to hell. He was twelve years old but he looked like he was nine, or eight, and his face was shriveled so small by something long and repeated you could fit it into your palm.

"Scrap," came the captain's voice which bellowed from the house and tore around its corners. The house was a faded green and had been pretty when Vincent's mother was alive, but she was long gone.

He rose to his feet and trudged around to the front that looked like a scrubby fallen warehouse and had dogs set out to protect it. This captain, whom Vincent considered an old man, was in his late forties, red-haired and skinny, with bulges of sinew on his neck and arms. Just now he was sullen and gruff but at other times, depending on what he was after, the old captain could make his voice do terrible things, rise high and wind-borne then come down gravelly before twisting to a cold, wet wire that wouldn't hardly twist unless he muscled it with his throat so hard Vincent could watch his eyes burn.

"Pull up some water, Scrap."

Vincent trudged out toward the bed of the truck, his leash unspooling from a spot just outside the door where the reel hung in a chipped plastic casement. He hove off a jerrican and let it drop the length of his arm then worked back up the hill to the house, lugging it while the water swished.

The old captain, whom folks who ventured that far up the mountain called Carl or just Cap, stood over the jerrican once Vincent had placed it in the dust before him and waddled inside with it squeezed between his insteps.

"You know what's coming tonight," the captain barked, with small eyes that came out from the fox sedge of his hair, then shut the door behind him.

Vincent returned to his bed where most nights he crept off to, spring through fall. The captain, before sleeping, would spool out the leash and, having given plenty of slack, run it twice around his arm. Then he'd lift his chair and weave the leash around both front legs so it made a noise, a dull rustle, when it tightened against the floorboards. And Vincent would slide out the door which never fully came to and head back around the house to the body-sized indent he'd dug in the dirt then filled with leaf litter from the sycamores once they'd given him leaves, or with moss which brought small bugs, or with the dry shag of an old rug the captain had allowed him to cut from its board.

Besides the captain and two of his trusted men, only Syd knew it. But the truth was the belt Vincent wore in that narrow hole, once it came tight around his waist a time and a half, curved down beneath his privates back up to his navel and was sewn again to the buckle. So he could shift it to relieve himself but he could never take it off.

"You should run for it, Vincent," Syd would tell him. She'd throw her thick bird's nest of hair back defiantly. "I'm the one who'll sure cut that leash."

Syd was older than Vincent by maybe a year, give or take. She had wild auburn hair and a broad-lipped smile and a distinctive smell like some young dogs, pleasant and wholesome, not fresh, but the odor of mushrooms you could get used to. He liked the way she'd hug him. He'd known only a few people. Maybe seven. Besides his mother, whom for some reason he could scarcely recall, Syd was the only one who had hugged him.

"He'll kill you, you know," Vincent would say back to her. "If you do that."

"He won't catch me," she'd whisper, shaking her head, laughing low and full of mystery, her warm belly moving beside him. "Now not with those hands."

The old captain had bad hands; it was true. Vincent didn't know exactly where they came from but only that they were hands from way back. The old man never spoke of them, and he hid the mangled stumps of his fingers, yet like most things over time they'd eventually come out. So Vincent would look sadly at Syd, at her light, sinewy body that to his worried eyes seemed to dance full of fear. Anybody could see, he'd think to himself, that the old man would catch her in an instant and throw her in his fall fire full of "scamp wood" built of dry tinder and slash which he burned for burning's sake, not to clear the ground of rot. Not for heat or light or to make space for his dogs, but out of pure malice.

Now, having lain for most of an hour in his burrow, Vincent was watching the sycamores blend with the sky and the growing dark that filled the holes in the woods until only the largest remained, gray and gaping, sawed into the horizon like an open barrel that hung in the air while everything, and most of all sounds, moved closer.

He was waiting, stock still, for Syd. Though he'd crane his ears for her, the first thing he heard more often than not was her soft, purring voice beside his ear. Generally, she came from the trees. She'd climb a yellowwood or a poplar, though this far up the mountain it was mainly stunted birch and sycamores alongside puny relatives of a gigantic beech growing down in the valley that here, in their scraggly forms far from the river, had reached the outskirts of their water range. The old man could hear a rustle sixty meters off and know, in no wind, if it was squirrel or deer. So Syd would come shyly, like a rabbit, through the duff. She'd crest the mountain from the south with the breezes off the lake normally in her face. And she'd take her time, so she said. Dipping into sage and fern and cutting wide of brambles. She'd stop when she was still far off from the dogs and get above them so she could survey the house.

Once, she'd told Vincent, when a dog had winded her, she'd stayed treed for several hours, maybe more than that, she couldn't say. But after dark, most of the dogs save one went in and slept by the captain on the boards around his feet, as though those scuffed, sheenless boards were sloping couches.

"Vincent," Syd would whisper once she'd already come fully to his ear. And Vincent had gotten so he could smell her warmth, even when she wasn't there. She'd come in and snuggle herself beside him until his berth was nearly large enough for two, worn down by those hours together. She'd stay late, sometimes past the frost, until it was sheer cold before she'd rise up and glide away from him out toward the trees and then, so he imagined, over the sawtooth crest of granite and in the pitch dark down the far side of the mountain into pastures. Finally, her knees wading through grass, she'd swing the gates at Denks Farm, or so he saw her in his mind, then climb the ladder into haymow and crawl into another bed, sagging from the rafters.

But Vincent had never witnessed any of this in person. For as long as he'd known Syd, which seemed long, he'd had eyes on only the house and the dogs and the captain, along with a brief stand of tulip poplars that, so the captain told him, had grown at the bidding of Vincent's mother along the back side of the house, farther from the sun, but now stood slack and derelict.

"He's put it out tonight's a hunt," Vincent warned Syd when she'd materialized at last and taken her place by his side. He stared at her, trying to make out her features which mooned large and strange so close to his eyes. From the time he'd met her, Vincent had known Syd as a country person knows an owl. In glimpses composed largely of darkness. As if seen from the slathering light of a barn or, once in a long while, in the shock of broad daylight when that owl comes loose from the trees with a sudden whoosh and for a moment, out in the woods, everything is falling.

Syd rarely came while the dogs were still out, which meant Vincent rarely saw her before sunset when he could still marvel at her shock of red hair, at how it took over most of her neck and flecked her face, even played in the corners of her mouth then scrambled down her back.

"This time you gotta run, Vincent. You can't just stay put."

"And where do you say I run to?"

"Anywhere. Anywhere you get's sure better than here."

"And how do you say I come clear of this?"

Vincent held out his leash which made a tight loop about his belt and was stitched heavily to itself in order to reinforce the solder point of its clasp with his buckle. The leash was mildly elasticized so that he curled it around a rock when he lay in his berth to give himself a length of slack before the captain had pulled it taut.

"Well, I might just cut it while he's out there on his dogs. When he can't just sick them on us here."

Vincent laughed softly. Not at Syd, who struck him as unreal. And not because she wasn't right. But at the thought of it, at the idea that anyone would ever take that chance. Or that he, Vincent, could ever do more than he was already doing, just by lying beside her, to put that girl in danger of her life.

Now Syd unsheathed a hunting knife, as she often did, that had been someone else's. She'd usually say first, before anything else, that it was her father's. "I can tell you this blade belonged to my father," she'd say, her voice even and serious.

Then, after a little while, when Vincent was quiet, "Well, I don't honestly say it was his, you know. One way or the other. But I can sure suppose."

If Vincent protested, or sought to question any of it, Syd would tell him that anyway he must be sick or crazy himself because no one would take what he took from that old man without running.

"You're only barely alive," she'd say softly. "Must be something's come loose in there." And she'd bring her head in close and touch it to his own, so that her hair was tousled around him, warm and thick as the woods. Until the fear that paralyzed Vincent, that left him fat-tongued and slow-footed and empty before the captain, would momentarily seep down from his eyes and, just for an instant, he could see things again.

Yet this time Syd didn't talk about the knife. She just held it up and brought it to bear on the leash and began to cut along the bias.

"Oh I don't think so," Vincent crooned, steadying her hand. "I wouldn't go and do that."

"And why not?" asked Syd. "I'm not afraid of his hounds."

"Oh no, I know," Vincent whispered. "I believe that."

But, truth was, he didn't.

•

The captain had started out on that mountain in the dog training business. He made tourist dogs, dogs from mining towns along the river, stray dogs and underfed sallow pups he himself picked up, mill dogs and litter mums whose teats dragged to the floor, into hunting dogs. Some time back, the Cap himself had been a hunter. He'd hunted for sport like the rest of them, playing in and out of seasons set down by law. But he'd grown outside of all that at some point, begun guiding people without licenses in the hills and mountains north of the Smokies, beyond the boundaries of the national park, in northeastern Tennessee. Then he'd come down to settle when a client bequeathed him some cheap land on a forested mountain, not far off from low-lying lakes formed long beforehand by the Tennessee Valley Authority when they'd begun constructing river dams back in the nineteen thirties.

By the eighties, however, the region had become almost exclusively fishing country, where locals who had money lived on man-made lakes and those who didn't scrounged digs in the woods and spent their money on bass boats. There were coyotes and an occasional wolf bachelor seeking a female, once in ten moons a black bear, but they were quickly run off or killed. Mainly it was whitetail deer and fox, some quail and dove, with little money in guiding. So the captain, once he'd lost his wife when she was still very young and hale, and then Vincent's mother had died in the prime of her life in what the captain called a "brush fire," turned to hunting his own dogs.

"In an ordinary operation," he'd explain to Vincent, "there'd be terriers or curs. You choose." He'd pause and study the wall. "Now there's bird dogs and game dogs. And you run either a straight retriever operation or a gundog rig, with pointers and hounds. One or the other. But damned if you'd see mutts or mastiffs like these."

The old captain would nod toward the dogs spread out at his feet and sigh when Vincent said nothing. He'd point with his elbow, as was his habit, at Vincent's dog, Chief, that was a broad-muzzled mutt. "Now see, Scrap, right here we've got us none of the above."

"Hands," he'd say then. And that meant that Vincent was to be the old man's hands. Vincent would jump to it, whatever it was, salting pork brought up from the valley by someone or other, or plugging holes big enough for wood moths in the calking along the ceiling, or taking off the man's pants for him after unlacing his boots.

"That's enough, that's good," the old captain would mutter. "That'a boy, Scrap. Just like that."

The truth was there were other things the captain made him do that Vincent hadn't spoken of to Syd. Concerning which, in fact, he'd said nothing to anyone.

•

"That man's an animal," Syd went on, now snuggling close. "An an-i-mal, I tell you." And she said the word slowly, from deep in the well of her throat, drawing it out. "C'mon now, wake up. You gotta get out while you can."

On hunting nights, the "clients," as the captain called them, would come up the hill in their Dodges and sport vans. They'd park them out front of the house and the captain would serve up beers and "meat steaks" that Vincent had made from venison sold in the valley and cooked on a rusted outdoor grill he pulled out from one of the lean-tos. The steaks were apparently tasty and required a good chaw and, so the men would tell one another, they got the blood flowing.

The bulk of the captain's dogs were split among three large kennels and individual cells sheltered in the lean-tos, and there were two types—those he used as hunters and were mainly bred, so he claimed, from hounds, and those that were an indescribable mix of blood which made them hungry for escape since, according to the Cap, they were "looking out for all those parts of themselves at once."

In general, the captain could talk dogs all day until Vincent would slink off and lie down. Then the old man would walk around one corner of the house and, still out of view, as though he didn't wish to look at Vincent at all, as though he didn't want to see him with his eyes, keep right on talking dogs.

"I know he'll send my Chief," Vincent told Syd while they lay there at the margin of the dim woods. “He’s threatened it,” and Vincent paused, deliberating. “So I know he will.”

“He shouldn’t hunt that animal,” Syd answered him. “That animal’s the last one should be hunted. I’d rather he hunted me.”

Vincent thought about Chief, piebald with a half-shut eye that hadn’t healed, walking always behind rather than out in front, growling low and deep when the captain approached, and during the long days, lying out back and keeping his one good eye locked on Vincent.

The fact was the old captain, once he’d bred a dog to be hunted, to take evasive action when put on the run, kept it apart from the rest and nearly starved it. He gave it sufficient strength to run on fear, but not enough grub to find safety in his keeping. After he’d given the hunting dogs its scent, he’d take it over the granite hulk of the mountain then partway down the back side and release it. Next, he’d travel a half kilometer or so to disguise the dog’s direction and blow a shrill whistle. Each client, riled, full of talk, with a hunting dog rented from the captain, would make off on foot. Not with rifles but with broad, plastic-hafted knives. And the trick of this kind of hunting, as the captain would explain, was to get close enough to finish the job while your quarry was alive. If you laid back and let your hunting dog do the work, then it was named a “no-hunt” and you’d face the derision of them all or, as the captain would say, “the whole thing came to a wasted dog.”

On hunting nights, the old captain would unspool Vincent’s leash all the way and say, “Hands,” and Vincent would key the locked reel while the old man watched and unlatch the leash outside the front door, bringing it around back where there was another housing constructed to fit neatly in the crotch of one of the poplars.

That housing was lashed to the tree until it stuck hard and made an indent, and on such nights the old man would have Vincent hook himself up at the back of the house. He was instructed to conceal himself and make no noise while the clients stayed inside or out front where their trucks stood steaming on a dirt track that ran down the mountain in crosscuts.

"That'll do for this evening, Scrap," the captain would say on such nights. "We'll just keep you back here, out of sight out of mind."

Syd, who'd been silent for some time, now walked over to the housing and inspected it, running her hand over it in the dark. She came back to the leash and wound it tightly about her wrist. Her mother's people, she'd told Vincent many times, had been Scottish homesteaders in the lowlands. But now they worked electronics jobs for Alcoa. Her father had been a backcountry woodsman who'd lived off the land and refused to mine the sand and loam for aluminum. He'd run off with her mother some years back and left Syd in the keeping of his brother who was himself a character she mentioned little and appeared eager to avoid. Not for long, she'd often told Vincent. Her folks wouldn't be gone for too long.

But tonight, Syd said nothing when she took her leave. She didn't linger with that air of hesitation he had come to love or tell him good night. For whatever reason, she didn't even whisper what she usually whispered on brisk dog hunt nights in the autumn, and that was that she supposed she'd better get on her way before the winds came up and she herself was the long-haired dog they were hunting.

•

Vincent lay still as the night deepened. He could hear the wavering calls of coyotes out in the hills above the lake. It must have gotten on, he reasoned, as he'd been watching the vague circuit of the moon for some time. It had risen late due to cloud cover and now was strangely far along for a dog hunt night. In fact, the captain, on such nights, was normally roving around. The leash would uncramp, and Vincent would be recruited to unlatch it from the front of the house and escort himself out back. Following that, he'd be kept busy with the venison and there would be "hands, hands" every few minutes.

"Scrap, no meat steaks tonight," came the captain's voice at last once it had grown very late. The old man stood well out of sight, where Vincent could see nothing at all in the dark but only hear the changeable voice that was high and wheedling.

"Why don't you come in now with me and your Chief."

Vincent rose reluctantly and trudged behind the captain who led the way into the house where his watchdogs already had taken their places before his chair and where Chief lay as always at night when he wasn't out with Vincent, alone on the far side of the room against the wall.

"Tonight, there's just two of 'em coming round." The old man paused. "So I thought you might just as well join in."

Vincent knew by this it was the trusted who would be there, two big men, hulking and slow, from whom the captain had not hidden his presence. They tended to look Vincent over as he stood before them in his reflective vest, in a way that made him feel small and vulnerable.

"And like I told you all along, Scrap, we'll be hunting your old mutt, Chief."

On hearing this, standing just inside the door, Vincent grew weak in the knees, as he had tended to do before the captain. It was a weakness that came with revulsion. With the knowledge that swept through him even before the hewn hands came out and roughed him. It was a weakness specifically that stood on the other end of those hands, as Vincent knew the calluses they bore and the strange cauliflower nodes of the bones and the pink, lingering cough of blood that lay floating just under the skin of them.

"Don't touch me," he whimpered. "I don't want you to touch me."

But the captain didn't seem to hear.

"Why don't you come over here, Scrap, and stop your yapping?" The voice cramped down on its wire until it grew thin and sharp.

"Hands," announced the captain but Vincent, who had just lain side by side with Syd, feeling the soft nudge of her shoulders and the warm stream of her breath—however long it had been, it didn't feel long—for once couldn't quite bring himself to do it.

"Now I need these pants off and on the floor," said the Captain, the voice tightening further.

But Vincent, who was only allowed to call the dog, Chief, his own because of things he'd done for the captain while the old man's pants were on the floor, things the captain called "favors," now that he heard the dog was to be hunted, couldn't bring himself to step across the cracked boards toward the man whose hands, mauled by something alive, no tool or machine—that was sure—were starting to come out from behind his back and stretch forward into the air.

"Now tonight I'm hunting that dog—less you do something about it."

"So then, afterward, if I do, you won't touch him," offered Vincent simply.

"And we'll just see about that when we get there."

The captain began moving forward, the hands shaped like crouching haunches without the full body of the animal.

"And won't we just look into it all, ol' Scrap?" he went on, drawling now, saliva thick, mouth open and tongue slow with the feet coming fast. "Later on."

But just at that point, there were lights streaking through the one pane in the southern wall. An engine coughed and quit. Then there was the long fixing of a parking brake and the stark huff of big men in cold air.

•

Syd lived with her uncle, as far as Vincent knew, on the same Denks Farm she'd talked about from the beginning. It had been two springs since Vincent's mother had died and in that time Syd had come more and more frequently up the mountain. She worked horses to earn her keep the way Vincent's mother herself had worked horses long before she'd met the captain, or so his mother had told him.

"Carl is not a man to have dealings with," his mother had explained to Vincent who at the time was still very young and had never come up the mountain from town. It was just she'd been thrown together with him out of a cruel necessity. And it was to be short-term, she assured anyone who'd listen, only long enough to get her bearings in the lake country. Yet when Vincent had been introduced finally to the captain, his mother had bid him sternly, with the old captain standing before them both, to heed all requests and help train the dogs. It was a good way to learn a trade, she'd explained, and like it or not, dog training was a thing you took along anywhere.

But his mother had brought Vincent down from Kentucky, from

the Cumberlands up north, and between the two of them they'd known nothing of any use, he'd long since decided. Because she'd died while she was still young and pretty, for no reason at all, and the captain's requests had changed over time, so that "hands," after his mother was gone, came to mean more than just lugging jugs and slicing duct tape or soaping buckets.

Now, when the first of the trusted, Dean, came in, slow and heavy, he looked at Vincent with evident surprise. And when Vincent turned to leave them to their business the captain called him back.

"Dean, we're setting on this one tonight," announced the captain and pointed to Chief.

"Please don't do it," said Vincent softly.

"Scrap's taken a fondness for him," explained the captain. "But I've got an idea to handle it."

"More often than not I find them two together out back of the house," he went on. And just then Steve, the other of the pair of big men, walked in, either having relieved himself or studied the weather.

"So I figure tonight we'll make Scrap here one of our hunting dogs."

Vincent stared at the captain vacantly, waiting for his meaning.

"I'll leash him up to my belt and see if he won't just bring that mutt to us."

At this, the captain walked past Vincent, pointing to the key he kept by his chair, and, having swung open the house door, he struggled to unspool the leash in its plastic housing. "Hands," he yelled, and once they'd all followed him, Vincent last, out into the night, the boy released the lock and unlatched his own leash and hooked it to Dean's belt as he was told.

Then the three men reentered the house with Vincent in tow and, having cornered Chief after a good deal of snarling and cuffing, they wrestled him at last into a heavy, scrim-backed dog bag striped against claw holes with electrical tape. They cinched it to at the end and lashed it around with heavy rope while Vincent watched by the door.

"Please," he mustered now and again, nearly inaudibly, standing slack-kneed across the room. But amidst the barking and scratching, and the subsequent banging with a cast-iron joining pipe, he could scarcely hear his own voice.

•

Vincent honestly didn't know if the captain had ever laid eyes on Syd. He believed the old man knew something was amiss, or that some stray outlier was escaping him in the slipstream of the woods, even if he couldn't exactly say that it was somebody, a girl with heavy hair, lying beside Vincent for an hour, sometimes two, at the start of cold nights. The fact was that Syd herself was a big talker, in whispers, and Vincent admired it, while believing little. Yet she taught him things she claimed to have learned from her father. And one of those things was you should never trust ignorance because people could sense what they couldn't name or know. Another was your ears in the woods were nearly always more valuable than your eyes. Syd, at the first sound, at the first hollowness in the air, at the soft curl of a breeze, would already be up and gone.

Now, left alone with the trusted while the old man hauled Chief, strapped to his back, out into the woods, Vincent stood shivering and thankful that Syd, as he figured it, was gone off to sleep in warm hay.

"Well, he ain't always been good to you, Scrap," murmured Dean. "That's for damned sure. But he aims to do right."

Steve, who must have thought this particularly mawkish, or pushing it a ways too far, coughed heavily and muttered, "Ah, bullshit he does. Cap hasn't changed one bit." Then he went on after a pause in which he stole a glance at Vincent's crumpled shoulders, "Unless he's gotten worse," with the result that Vincent was momentarily confused about allegiances, about who was trusted by whom.

For a long time, the three of them waited for the whistle and when it came far off to the south, beyond the back side of the mountain away from the lake toward Denks Farm, they started with the dogs out ahead and Steve in the rear and Dean, who hadn't hardly spoken before, now talking a river, mainly about the old captain, about how he'd been a crack shot in his day but had turned cunning by necessity and could find a buck doubled back or traipsing through streams or, for that matter, track a lone doe carried down willy-nilly, neck-high in a flood.

"How'd in hell he do that, swim without hands?" hissed Steve who began laughing quietly, perhaps derisively, until Vincent felt he could hear behind him soft round shoulders full of beer and venison shaking in the woods, and without so much as looking back, glimpse in his mind that big, bearded head of Steve's with its stained, neutral eyes, rocking in the darkness.

"No, I don't think so," finished that same voice behind, grown suddenly stern and grim.

After the captain had whistled twice more, they found each other not far from the house. The captain said "hands" and Vincent switched the leash until anywhere the old captain went he came following behind him through the dark trees. The leash was only partially spooled out, to perhaps twelve feet, and Vincent had never had it quite like this, where he was trailing with little slack and straining in the near dark to see how the old man ducked and turned so he could dodge the same stunted birches and toppled storm debris and deep pockets of leaf litter. They had separated so that, at Steve's insistence, the trusted went off individually and Vincent and the old man kept moving swiftly, covering ground, following "them mutt hounds" now well out ahead until they'd crested the granite top of the mountain and begun down the back side.

After what seemed to Vincent a long time, but may have been less than an hour, the captain halted abruptly, and the leash went slack and dropped. Vincent himself stopped and listened. He recalled Syd noting in one of her whispers what she'd learned from her father, that the most dangerous time for traveling in broad-leafed woods was late in the autumn before the snows when there was less natural cover and the leaves had curled and anything moving on the ground, however light and fleet, made three, four times the noise.

The captain recommenced his march and suddenly halted again. He turned and stepped back toward Vincent. His hands came out partway in the dark then thrust forward abruptly. Vincent felt them on his body, rough and insistent. After a moment, the old man shifted behind him and seemed to be listening, peering out into the woods up the grade they'd just descended.

When at last the captain began again to move down the mountain, he did so more slowly, as though cautiously, traveling without hands or the trusted, as if, for the first time Vincent could recall, with fear in him. The dogs were now almost beyond their hearing but seemed just then to be turning, strangely, in a distant loop to the east back up the slopes toward the house. Vincent, who'd felt hot and weak throughout and struggled to keep pace, his legs slow and leaden, continued to dwell morbidly on Chief that had been his mother's dog, thick-jawed, slender at the haunch, before he was his. The dog had taken to Syd the way he'd taken to Vincent, and yet, until the first frost, he wouldn't lie down next to either of them in the berth in the back of the house but only at a distance, watching intently from the poor cover of the first sycamores a stone's throw away.

Just then, something came from behind, as if from nowhere, and touched Vincent near the ear. Next there was the warm, acrid smell of its hand over his mouth, so he grunted and for an instant began to struggle. His first thought was it belonged to one of the trusted, who were surely the only souls about, as all along he'd been waiting for Dean in particular to hurt him somehow as he marched through the dark woods. But the hand was damp and bony, small, and he could feel individual fingers pressed against his lips. In another moment, with astonishing quickness, whatever it was had wedged itself in front of him and was bent over the leash, furiously working an arm. Having been halted entirely, Vincent wavered for a moment then lurched free, stumbling backward, and was suddenly standing on his own.

The old man, who'd been jerked off his pace, cried back to Vincent, "Goddamn Scrap, you fall on your face?"

But Vincent didn't answer. He was mesmerized. The same small form was still standing very close in the dark, hunched by a tree. It had taken the slack from the leash and was winding it powerfully around the bole, making laps then tucking it down through. While he himself struggled to keep his feet beneath him, and while the time thumped like a dog or a coyote in his chest, Vincent could dimly make out, since it was all so close beside him, that the figure was using its mouth and swiftly bringing a knot to, crouched low and yanking with its teeth.

"You can't save your goddamn mutt by dawdling," bellowed the old man who came hauling up the incline, stumbling over uneven ground unlike what they'd covered before, thick with duff and tangled bramble and loose talus, as if it had been specifically chosen for its roughness.

"He's good as dead," rose that sheer voice shimmying closer as if along a thin wire. "Guarantee, those boys will set on that dog."

But just then Vincent felt her arms on him, as she'd come up whirring from the bole. He shrunk back, despite the fact he knew already in his stupor it wasn't Dean but Syd, had known it from just after the moment she'd touched him, because as much as she'd whispered about the importance of his ears, Vincent could always smell her until he himself and even Chief smelled like that. And it was the one thing, he'd believed now for years, that had kept him so long alive.

"Run, Vincent," came her voice, straining pure and fierce above the captain's as though the woods were going up in flame, and all at once she was heaving on his wrist, spitting into his eyes, her hair in that fast madness spreading over his face. As if for all those nights lying beside him—by now she'd somehow hoisted Vincent half onto one shoulder, was staggering beneath his weight—that strange girl had been telling him the truth.

For another block of seconds as she half dragged, half carried his body across the grade, Vincent remained limp while something stirred in his craw, a far distant thrashing so long asleep it would not quite explode. But since that girl had infused him with such a panicked burst of life, he filled those instants, before he did anything, with the searing thought that Steve might just have gotten there first and turned those dogs, that Chief might still be alive, and if he could only budge his stalled-out legs there was perhaps some other mountain, he didn't know, where the captain, try as he might, would fail to track them.

All this time, Vincent felt her alive and powerful beneath him. Moaning under her burden, crumpling to the earth then rising again, screaming into the woods the oldest word, and, with the strength of a hidden animal, hauling him into existence.

"Run!"

THE NIGHT SHADES OF THE OCEAN

I.

When they found the money, they looked at each other silently and he went up for gloves.

She had already, in so many words, said "if we find it, best to say nothing." They'd leave it where it was, if it was hidden at all, for as long as they lived in the rental. Then a year on, two years, assuming it was still around, they'd stuff it in the bottom of a box with all the storage and pack out.

She stayed put in the cellar while he went up to their small apartment to retrieve the ski glove liners he never wore. When he came back down, he pulled out the plastic bag wedged in a pipe crook deep under rotting plywood, tucked in a damp corner where spiders hung from their own gallows. Something was inside the plastic bag, beige, a bursar's purse. He unsnapped it and bills stacked into view, not crisp but not faded either, in neat packets the way they're loaded, everyone suspects, into armored security trucks.

He was the one who found the money, but she'd gotten them looking in the first place. And while there were seven packets, he counted just one, his voice a soft current across his lips. At one point he murmured, "Seventeen thousand," and still in the packet, "Thirty-nine."

"All right, something like two fifty, two seventy-five," he said. "Talking serious money."

She nodded in concentration, shifting her weight toward the plywood, coming onto her toes.

"Well—had to be more than *that*," she breathed and began slowly to wedge her small, tight body so far into the wall as to merge with the pipe structure.

•

The fact was he'd been doing his homework that afternoon for a second-year graduate class on animal behavior when the intruder came through. He'd gotten up for the bathroom. When he made it back to the windows baying out beside the table there were cop cars out front. Six of them. Maybe eleven cops. All of them away from their vehicles, milling beyond the front door of the three-story apartment building for students. It contained three snug apartments, one on each floor, narrowly aligned so each had a kitchen and bathroom in back and a long hallway out to the living area fronting the street. A bedroom ran alongside the hall, wide enough for a double bed.

"Damn," he'd blurted out. "What the hell's this?"

At the time, he was in shorts and a T-shirt, despite the cold, so he threw on a jacket and came out the back door, talking to cops who didn't know much, and to cops who wouldn't say much, and to cops who talked like it was lunch. Big cops, basically all fat, standing more or less 6'1", rolled up tight in their clothes, proud of their rolls and badges as though they'd come fresh from winning themselves at a bake fest. He himself was just under six feet and sinewy, taut, so it was a skipjack talking to whales.

Two women showed up in blazers and expensive hair, serious. They walked around fast with long insect gaits. Everyone was checking over fences and behind things, even behind themselves. They were looking for a hat, which must have been a mask, because somebody said "hat" and one of the expensive ladies asked for a color then rapidly brought her hands over her face, opening spaces between her pointers and thumbs. The whales pulled trash can lids and stuck their heads in. They panned out and combed bushes that lined the long alley before it dead-ended in peaked shrubs caving to tamped winter grass. Because none could climb fences, they clomped the long way around in shiny, heeled boots.

"Bank robber," said one of them, pointing at the guy standing cuffed in front of the house. White guy. Around his own height—5'11". The paddy wagon already idling just behind. A whale on each side. The guy's head bowed. Looking like everybody looks on the street except cops. Like he himself looked. Longish dark hair. Dropped shoulders.

The guy never fully looked up, which was good. They never made eye contact. He didn't want this thief, who by now he understood from the cops had gotten in the third floor then traveled down the inner stairs to the cellar, to see his own face which, from all he could make out, was practically the same face.

II.

Later that night, she decided she would be right to keep the money. There was nothing they had to make her feel she shouldn't. It sure wasn't like she had that kind of money now.

He was thinking, she imagined, when they'd gone off to bed and were lying a good foot and a half apart at the edges of the mattress, it's no mistake you can make. Stealing other things is bad, but sometimes people forget. Steal money, though, then everybody remembers—so take something else if they're going to catch you. She could hear the grooved hum of his brain. It would be like him to get stuck on those things.

But after he'd twitched and gone silent, slipping down into sleep, she was still there. And for a while, maybe a whole minute, she thought she could kill him.

Weird, she thought, where'd that come from? Why in hell would I do that?

•

The cops came next day to talk to the girl upstairs.

"They talk to you too?" asked the girl that evening, having knocked on their door.

"Who?"

"Those police."

"We weren't here," he said.

"Oh, well they talked to me. For a long time. All this about who do I know and why he got in my apartment instead of the first floor." The girl toed the draggled fringe of the carpet. "Or yours."

"Officers?" she demanded from the sagging couch on the far side of the room.

"Officers?"

"Officers asking you all that?"

"Oh no, it was a woman with them. Two police, and she was the detective. Going on about how he made it down cellar to hide."

"Why don't you come in," he said finally.

After a while, the girl went back upstairs and he admitted the whole thing was getting him tired.

"It's our second day," she said. "Day two. You haven't *done* anything yet."

•

They opted not to go down that night to see if the cops found the money. She thought it best to hold off a few days. If the cops didn't find it they'd come again, until they did find it. So smarter to wait it out.

Actually, over the course of the ensuing weeks, those cops might have come many times for all she knew. She told herself by and large she was over the whole thing. She'd been busy with a project at the university's extension school where she was a part-time, returning student looking to finish up her bachelor's degree in psychology. She'd left college a year and a half before graduating to go traveling for a semester, then hadn't gone back. Nor had she traveled beyond the confines of the state of California. After a year, on a lark, she'd split the gas and accompanied a girlfriend on a road trip to the East Coast. The girlfriend had since returned west. But she'd stayed on in Boston as two more years went by.

When she met her fiancé at a bar outside the university quadrangle, she'd thought she could finally see eye to eye with somebody serious, who was going places. So she opted to buckle down and finish the degree she'd started out west. "Only four more semesters at this rate," he'd reminded her in his protective way. But her secretarial job took most of her time and it was such slow going, only one course per term, with tuition rates for individual courses so high. Hard to keep her head up. So now, after a while, when things got real quiet, she allowed herself again to muse about the money.

"Anyway, doesn't somebody have to let the cops in?" she asked him at one point.

"Sure, but Real Estate lets them in," he replied, referring to the university office that managed the apartments.

Then, when it had been just about three weeks, they went down to check the money. The bag was still there. She looked around, according to what they'd decided in advance, for cameras, or audio detection, anything planted in the cellar, before she reached all the way back into the wall and brought the plastic bag, now stained with rust and grime, out from the crook in the pipe.

Still seven packets. Fat as ever. She wore his soft glove liners and she didn't count. She showed him the contents of the purse, oblong and cracked, a false leather, then replaced it in the crook of the pipe behind the plywood. The plywood, rotting at its corners, looked untouched.

"Fools," she whispered.

And this time, after he'd fallen asleep, she thought if she had the money in fifty years, or whenever it happened, and he died first, leaving her utterly alone, she would give him the most princely funeral. She would invite everybody they knew, even her mother, if for whatever reason her mother managed to stay so long alive.

III.

"Hey," he called out when he came home.

She was sitting at the chipped, lacquered table near the bay window where they ate, shades drawn, counting money with her bare fingers. Going through stacks.

"What the hell are you doing now?"

"Counting."

"Why the hell you have it up here?"

"Christmas."

He stopped walking toward her. It was twenty-something days, barely more than three weeks, and she was pawing the money. Son of a bitch.

"Listen, you've got to talk before you do something like this. You're screwing us both."

"By buying people their Christmas presents."

"We've got money saved up for that."

She snorted. "You're blowing my count."

"All right, so while you're at it, he posted bail." This, at least, he managed to say softly. "Checked again this morning."

She brought her eyes briefly to his like there was something he might be holding back. "Fine," she said. "Good thing then I brought up the money."

"You know he won't send somebody. He'll come himself."

She nodded absently, her lips gliding over big numbers as if they bore exotic names.

"Then when he gets in, and it's not there, he thinks us. We've got all the junk stored. With our names right on the boxes. So we must go down there. So we're the ones found the money."

"Nope. He thinks cops first. Normal cops find the money. If not them, gas people since furnaces get checked. Or cleaners, with hall mops blocking up the stairs. Maintenance probably, down with boards and their stubby pencils—all those empties rolled out."

She was rattling on calmly, with an unusual air of self-assurance. "I put in a date on the far furnace log when I was down there. For December 9. So you know."

"He won't see that."

"Could though. Then moved the Camel pack with those two-by-fours over near the corner."

"And what about your prints?"

But he could tell she'd wandered back into the money. For a long splice of slow time he stood there counting along with her in fixed concentration from out in the middle of the room, losing the smallest amount of feeling in his knees.

"Right, so nobody's checking two-by-fours," she said at the end of the thick stack. She clacked it down on the table. "It's *our* fucking apartment. We can touch things."

IV.

That night, she was sad she had ever, even for a minute, thought of killing him. It wasn't over the money, she was positive. Just something out of the blue. From time to time you come up with anything. Who knows why? Sure can't ask around.

But now it had happened, she couldn't exactly forget. Best thing to do, if she ever started feeling that same way again, was take off. Do what everyone else did in touch-and-go situations. Why reinvent the wheel? Take the money and her sweet ass to some other country.

After all, it's three hundred ten grand, she was thinking, having lied to him earlier that night about the total. She'd told herself he could go count it out himself, but she was pretty sure he wouldn't. Always insanely suspicious of others and way too trusting of her. He'd drop everything and protect her to the ends of the earth. It was a gene. Or just stubbornness. Anyway, you know a few things about your man, or he hasn't ever been yours.

"Is that your guy?" she asked a couple of days later, watching now nearly all the time, moving from one window to the next, especially at night, then collapsing back on the sofa, avoiding windows. Then getting up to peek out again.

Sure enough, on Saturday morning, five days before Christmas, in the broadest daylight, it was no false alarm.

"Damn," he said, backing away from the bay windows.

"Him all right."

"*Does* look a hell of a lot like you."

They watched him prowl around.

"Guess he'll head around to the porches where he got in on the day. Then circle back and check out pizza fliers. Bet he picks one up then tries the front door."

"So unlock it." She could feel the sweat beading. Her sweat, before it came on full blast, typically pearled on her temples and collected along the inquisitive curve of her eyebrows that were sexy, he'd assured her, drop-dead.

"Wait, what?" His hands floated into the morass of his raven-dark, shoulder-length hair.

"If he does go around, like you're so sure, unlock down front while he's back there."

"But why in hell would I do that?"

"'Cause then he sees for himself the money's all gone."

He stared at her. First, from what she could tell, at her mouth. Then, at her narrowly set eyes which, according to the mirror, came off pleading. Like she was hoping for something a little too hard. In those moments, taking herself in, she'd tried picturing a desert island where, in two months at the outside, she would have her own names for all the night shades of the ocean.

Now she edged closer to the blinds. She had them slatted just right, so she didn't need to pry them open with her fingers. So there'd be no bulge.

"Where's he at now?"

"Gone."

He turned to open the apartment door and she crept onto the landing to watch his long, slender toes go bloodless as they eased down rubber silencers on the inner stairs.

When he was back up and she'd returned to the blinds, she pushed the air down with her palms, motioning quiet. She watched as the sonofabitch in his faded blue Patagonia vanished onto the covered stoop beneath them before, after six minutes, exiting the front door of the building to make off toward town, striding.

"See," she said afterward, while they drank wine from a wine-sized bottle. Not a carton or a jug. "Maybe now he won't come back—maybe that was what it took."

"You spend the money on this wine?"

"I spent money."

"Not at that store down the road."

"Nope. But I didn't truck it to Timbuktu."

And that night, she lay in their bed on her stomach like a lioness with paws out front of her chin. "We should go to Africa," she said softly to the room while he slept. Damned right, she thought. We should put on tan clothes and hats with air holes and go on safari. But before she could sleep into those plains, into the dry, wide breadth of the Serengeti, she'd turned her hunting rifle on him from in tight, with his quiet, slender face there in ridiculous close range, the small bump on the bridge of his nose big and blurred in her sights, and still, after long seconds drifted by, not pulling the trigger. Then, this time, pulling the trigger.

V.

The whales showed up just after the first full moon of the new year and milled around the cellar. Then the bastards came up to ask questions. She'd spent on groceries for some time. It was aggravating to be this exposed, with her out there at large. Taking subways, sure, like they'd agreed; changing stores each time, as if that did anything when they were calling bill numbers. The food tasted good though. It looked all golden and round, the chicken especially, and they took more time over dinner together. He had the low-grade stipend from school, just enough to cover discount rent, and her small salary sourced lentils and bulgur from the bulk section. But now, for three weeks running, he'd devoured a lion's share of meat.

"We'd like to ask a few questions about events in late November."

"What events?" she asked.

"Pertaining to the break-in at this building."

"You want the third floor."

"Come on in," he told the cops.

One of the women with the getup, in sharply creased pants, was lurking a step back. Then, once inside, the detective explained from out of her hair, stiff as a clamshell around her face, there remained "outstanding issues in the case." Monitoring her posture, resisting the collapsed sofa, she piled on additional bland, morbid phrases. How there was "an ongoing investigation." How their "cooperation might be necessary."

Afterward, he told her they were screwed. "See, they're onto us, girl."

"Standard run-through," she said, eyes traveling casually back from the bay window. "The bitch has just watched too many shows."

That night or the next one, in the dark, she must have taken the money out of the drawer and hidden it. But she wouldn't say where.

"You're slowly betraying me," he told her.

She smirked. "Sure, right—by saving your narrow ass."

"And how is that saving?"

She sat hunched over the table, face comically scrunched in thought.

"Then my fault when they catch us."

"So why the hell we doing it?"

"*You*'re not."

A few weeks later, in February, just before Presidents' Day, when she'd been touting the advantages of taking a long weekend to spend the money far away and he'd thought too risky—"They'll put our movement with the money's, that's worse than spending it next door"—the cops returned, this time without the woman with thick mascara and dolled hair.

"Same ones again," he said. "Right out front."

"Then let 'em come in—I've got nothing to hide."

Accompanying one of the whales was the small guy with squinting monk's eyes who had studied them before as they'd listened to the detective drone on. His was the foreboding stare of someone who'd seen the same thing again and again and knew exactly what it looked like.

Now there was a warrant to search. Having let both in, they were escorted by one whale out to the back porch while the squinty-eyed monk searched with two more cops waiting downstairs. They sat on the porch for fifty minutes with the whale who kept his gaze fixed on the peeling gray clapboard somewhere just to the right and above the tops of their heads.

When the cops all finally emerged onto the porch, the small, monkish guy, last out, nodded wanly and gave them permission to return. There was something ominous about the way his eyes lingered on their faces. Especially on hers. His looking seemed to come out from a deep place of puzzles silently crammed together.

"Lucky I'm so inventive," she said once everybody was gone.

"How you know they haven't bugged us?"

"Seriously, though. Who'd bug this place—we're small fry."

He smiled at her. She was evidently having fun. She'd brought her hair into a neat coil that was beautiful, and she was moving fast, prying up cushions and probing behind shelves.

"You're a small fry," he said. Then, more quietly, "And, you know, still mine."

VI.

That night, after he was asleep, she got up from bed and padded in her woolen socks back to the kitchen. She opened, in the cold, the window giving onto their frosted winter garden and climbed into the leafless sugar maple that grew beside the apartment house. Its limbs had bent to the contour of the wall and, above her head, they bent again at the level of the sloped roof where they stretched from near vertical, freed at last by space, to flare out above the moldering shingles.

The money was in a blackened cavity in the bole where, like a marten, she had hidden things before. She'd reinforced the bursar's pouch with two plastic bags, then traveled out to it nights. There was a crossing where she could walk upright along the rough maple branch and balance with her hands spread into the wind. Plumb with the second story, it was above where a body would want to fall, and she wavered only because nobody, she imagined, walks perfectly straight.

"Cold, cold," she murmured, having reached the trunk and monkeyed up toward the crown above roof level. The stark wind hollowed the sky and left it empty and bright. Balancing in her socks, she could see down through blue darkness an inch or two into the tight room where, no doubt, he was stretched out in their bed. Somewhere inside he was lying there, quiet, beside towers of used paperbacks and her snow globe of a deer in storm, and two ragged bears from their childhoods. Just by the window, an enduring aloe plant they'd bought together arced green and tentacular into the dry air.

"So you suspect us two of being bank robbers then?" she'd asked the cop on the porch.

But the "whale," as her fiancé liked to refer to them, had ignored her. "Damned fools," she murmured now above the roofs. Having tightroped out again midway between the house and the broad bole of the frozen sugar maple, higher now, above the money, above even the crest of the roof shingles, she let go of the branches and spread her arms. Then stuffed out her chest and prepared to drop. She swayed there a moment, shut her eyes, and slung open her jaw, breathing.

Even though she'd bet herself she couldn't keep her eyes sealed, she did. She swanned forward, hands tingling, mouth hot. But as her face and shoulders began to slip through the air, when briefly she came free and kited into the darkness, she suddenly arched backward, twisting then yanking in her hips. She threw out her arms to grab hold of the limb her feet had rested on, chest grazing it, sliding off. Then before she could stop herself, she was wrapping her body madly around that same wide maple branch, fingers splaying into the cold grooves of its bark until, in the end, she was hanging by her legs and arms beneath it.

When she opened her eyes and craned her neck, she could just make out the ground through the cage of bare limbs far below in the black-and-blue night, and she shimmied back toward the trunk. She pulled the money out from the cavity then walked with it airily toward the window, one arm thrust forth to balance the other with the cash.

Inside, back in bed, a little bloodied from the maple, she tucked the money safely between them, still in all its bags. For a long time, half the night, she was awake. Then, in the morning, hair swung out front and holding a sheen she liked seeing, she went to the mall in the suburbs by commuter rail and bought a thick, stuffed coat—coffee-colored, same as her hair—that hung below her knees and was warm as the sultan's bath.

VII.

He decided while she was gone to take the money—what was left of it, which was still most—to the river. She'll be angry for a while, he mused, but it was never ours to keep. Sooner or later, before too long, whales will find it, she's right about that. We've had our fun.

Though, when he thought it over, the fun had never been his. Even so, at the moment she returned, he was buried in his studies, deep in an article on rich, dark Amazonian soils, while the money on the table was a dragon's brooch smoldering in slanted winter light.

"You were going to throw it out," she said. "Weren't you?"

"Nope."

"It's okay—I left it for that. Now I'm surprised you did nothing."

"You would never have forgiven me."

"Sure—I'd be disappointed."

"Then?"

"Probably rob my own bank." She smiled at him without frowns, with an openness, an effortless calm, he could scarcely remember seeing in her before.

"Or killed me," he said quietly, and her eyes darted over to his.

"Could, too, if I wanted," she laughed in the sumptuous fervor of her new coat, all of her suddenly alight, trembling. "Go on believe that."

They went out for dinner, the expensive kind, to a place they often traipsed past, staring a few feet through its latticed windows. It serviced professors and financiers and the wealthy undergraduates on whispering, low-lit dates. Though just down the street, they drank wine there with someone else pouring, smiling at the smallest things. Toasting loudly. Like they did those kinds of things all the time.

"Now that's a vintage," he said at some point, late in the bottle, and she laughed deeply and called him "baby" which she only did when she got buzzed. In the flickering candlelight, he could see the wide space between her two front teeth that, for some reason, had first made him raw for her and, for several months, even after they had been together, left him stuttering a little, as he'd done a whole year when he was a kid. She would reach over, during that period, and touch him somewhere, softly on the shoulder or the leg, to let him know she was close. That she understood there were hardships, even in the center of joy.

VIII.

That night, she lay in their bed, the money on the table within reach of her hand. Sheets pulled up to her waist. When she couldn't sleep, she slipped on her frayed jeans and lifted first the kitchen window then the storm. She went out walking in the maple, counting the times she'd gone back and forth between the sill and the bole over a lane of wrinkled bark. At one point, she buried her hand, balled to a fist, in the empty crevice of the tree. Then rolled it around inside the cavity, touching everything. *Nice,* she mused, when there was nothing there at all.

On the fourth crossing, near the smooth burl that served as a midstation, she asked aloud, "And why would I kill anybody?" That was obviously never real. Just tonight, he'd sworn he loved her, not once but many times. Sure, he was talking wine. But truth was she'd never hurt a soul. There were a few sere, claw-shaped leaves chirring among the rough branches. Leftovers. Stragglers. Scratching at the forager wind. No bundle of money could be worth all this.

Relieved, frozen through, she crept in, thinking in another season she'd be coated in sugar. As it was—but her thoughts gave out while she shivered, her shoulders in their bed still trembling, still soft and glossy from the moon for, if she had to guess, close to twenty minutes.

IX.

The whales, just as he expected of whales, came within seven days of the warrant search. By then, he'd wiped the money down and placed it in its bursar's pouch, then wiped that. Using gloves, he'd returned the whole diminished package to its original plastic bag and stuck it back in the crook of the pipe structure behind rotting plywood.

"Wiping won't do it," he'd said sadly, feeling a distant unease once it was tucked away. As though something beyond just cops—rangier, more desperate—were tracking them from afar. "If they've got something on us, you know, video log, a physical description." But he trailed off and thought only to scour the horizon. "They'll set up their big camp," he added quietly. "They'll find your money."

"Oh nice, okay—so now it's *my* money."

And since they'd rehearsed their story, staying up nights with wine, he said nothing when his eyes lifted from forest predation charts to the sight of patrol cars. He motioned to her and they stood like tall owls at the long table across from one another, waiting for the buzzer.

But just as the whales approached the stoop, she stepped to a hair's breadth of his chest and whispered something fast he asked her to repeat. She slurred it the second time, as if her lips slid through dreams slung too deeply within her to trick out with words.

"Wait, what? Hold on, what's this?"

"Exactly—so keep them off three minutes and I'm out of your way."

He stood staring down mutely into the wash of her hot metal breath. There, nearly grazing his toes, were her unlaced Pumas making massive two scrawny, splayed-out feet.

"Fine, thirty seconds—least do that."

When the buzzer stung him, she was gliding toward the back door, and he was lagging far behind. Legs gone stupid. Buckling animals inside. The blood in his ears a dark ocean in storm.

“I’ll go back out the front ’cause I’ve got to,” she murmured, so it came off rote like the start of a prayer. Her delicate hand—one part that stayed tender and possible—pointed down through the floor toward the money in the cellar. “Then haul out with it for the alley.”

“Look, no, c’mon. We’re still good here. C’mon.”

On the far side of the kitchen, beyond a windfall of fruit from the fancier market across the winter river, she shut her eyes. She bowed her head, just a little, then lifted her face so it was calm and young. Untouched by the cold of blue midnights when he’d seen her with the money out in the sugar maple. It dawned on him she’d been fighting herself during all those sorrow hours of the moon. And that she’d made it through. She was in the life.

Then she smiled like she’d smiled before they learned each other’s names.

“Right. Yeah—because I’m *saving* you, baby.”

LEVIATHAN

None is so fierce that he dare stir him up.—Job 41:10

The house was small and got you used to bird life. There were mynahs most of all, common mynahs, roosting in mating pairs in the winter and in large flocks in the springs and summers on the beach. They had bright yellow beaks with banded white tails showing smartly from behind when they were on the wing. In addition, the *honu*, or Hawaiian green sea turtle, would draw itself out of the sea and gradually turn the color of lava that had cooled and sat for years beneath the sun. A brown color once black which became, in the brightness of noon, hard to see at all.

Whole lives had been lived like this, for all Cal knew. The aromatic calm formed an unwavering picture in his mind, and since he'd been a child on family visits to the island, roaming the inlets of lava on the beach, he had understood the ocean in only one way, as something slow and warm with enduring comforts. Occasionally it occurred to Cal that in winter, while he was on the mainland, there were storms. But he pushed this knowledge away.

Now he crept quietly off the lanai onto the beach. The sand, even at this late hour, was hot and the heat seeped into the pads of his feet and made him hasten toward the water. He stood perched on the lava looking not at the ocean but toward the house, toward Harold, who was round at the belly and lay back asleep, his head lolling with the startled fury of the beard gushing massive and wild, until it was the thing most conspicuous from the tide line.

Harold was new to the sea, comparatively, though they'd been coming to the house Cal had inherited from his mother, a rich San Diego dowager of the 1960s, for twenty years together now. The sea still seemed to mesmerize Harold who hailed from Ohio and belonged to lakes and ponds. Warm summer ponds you could approach via long wooden jetties and, as Harold told it, you could splash into, with gaping strides through the air, in your youth. Cal had the impression when Harold spoke of these things that it was still possible to be young, that it was a place rather than a time, and one, moreover, you could still travel toward if you sought ardently the desires that had lived there.

In any case, Harold had never swum in the water in Hawaii. He'd dipped his toes, sure; he'd responded to coaxing by laying his considerable bulk in the tide pools, yes; he'd been nibbled by tiny, carnivorous glass shrimp, nearly translucent, and by juvenile raccoon butterfly fish. But he had never swum out with Cal to the drop-off where occasionally you glimpsed large pelagics, a spotted eagle ray flying with her calf, a pod of spinner dolphins swallowing long circles of rest or, very rarely, a whitetip reef shark cruising the bottom structures, seeking then finding a ledge of coral under which to pause and drowse.

Nonetheless, Harold was clearly intrigued by large predators and sea mammals. Dolphins intrigued him. It was rare that dolphins visited the bay in their languorous sweeps of the shoreline but occasionally Cal would hear Harold exclaim. Then his lover would point vigorously, eyes squinting with the brush line of his brows buckling. "Spinners," he'd mutter a second time, collecting himself, in a voice that was calm and flat, belying his excitement.

"In that case, why don't we take the kayak?" Cal would watch Harold carefully in such moments, wondering if he was tempted, knowing him to be unwilling to don a mask and sink his broad body into the ocean.

"Oh, they'll be long gone," Harold would say quickly. Or, "No need to disturb their rest."

Even so, Harold had clearly become a student of spinners, of the way they hunted at night and rested and bonded in their long circles during the days. They were smaller than bottlenose dolphins, more athletic, and Harold would watch them spin out of the sea then crash back down with resounding slaps of what seemed to Cal like pure joy.

"Status and power," Harold would correct him. "They're either hunting or making displays." Then Harold would drone on in dry monotone about impressing mates, territorial war, and bachelor factions shaking the structures of dolphin authority. He was really quite knowledgeable, Cal thought, for a man who never ventured into the water. Cal himself knew only what it was to swim beside a pod of spinners thirty feet down, to look them in the large eye that was deeply far from the end of the nose, to see the bright white gleam beneath the gray of their flesh, and to feel them slow and patient beside him, as though awaiting the long curving strokes of his fins. The dolphins, with calves gliding silently beneath mothers' bellies, with the thickness of their bodies slimming to thread whitely into broad tails, were the muscles of the sea, their gazes entering you through water and growing inside your lungs until you were forced to turn up for air.

•

Cal turned at last from Harold toward the water and scanned the bay. It was choppy with a seaward breeze that pushed at the incoming tide and made humps like the backs of things. This whole expanse, the ocean, would not make sense without the lanai and the stand of coconut palms he and his mother had planted and that now tilted and rattled in the wind. Nor would the placid bay live at all for him without the old man snoring in his chair. How could that be? Harold who never went into the sea. If it were up to Cal, after all, one would hardly get out of the ocean—

"Shark," yelled Harold from behind him.

"What?" Cal turned to face the lanai and Harold was standing, staggering, then descending unsteadily onto the beach.

"Shark," he yelled again, this time pointing with his whole giant hand as though it were a ventral fin, the thumb tucked in, palm downturned and level with the ground.

"Where?"

"There. Past the surge zone. Coming back in. That's a big one now. Huge one."

Cal turned and stared.

"Never seen one like that." Harold was hoarse, bellowing. Burbling on. Coming up sweaty and grabbing him by the shoulders, roughing him in his excitement so that Cal, who was lithe and tall, nearly fell down.

"See it," said Cal, straightening himself. "That does look large."

The dorsal indeed stretched surprisingly high off the surface, was wide at the base, and swiveled slightly, aggressively, in a way that Cal had never seen.

"Big sucker," whispered Harold, clearly fascinated. Now they could make out a shape beneath the water, again, surprisingly large, of a scale Cal had only seen in a young whale, in humpback calves he'd dived with off the northern coast of the island, near Hawi.

"Jesus Christ," blurted Harold excitedly. At last, the shark was close enough to the shore that they could see, squinting out across the lava breaks, that the dorsal was mottled, even banded at its base with jagged swaths of shadow crossing the blade. "Christ, that's a tiger."

Cal twisted free of Harold and ran to the side of the house. He grabbed the light hawser of the kayak and started hauling, running with it as best he could down the beach to the break and finally dipping the bow into the first crust of the waves.

"Get in here, Harold," he hollered, expecting Harold to begin shuffling backward as he invariably did when challenged, to start shifting his bulky shoulders in retreat, tracing a line with his heels up the beach toward the lanai.

But Harold stood transfixed and Cal, turning quickly, could see the outline of the shark clearly now, the sun cutting across it from the west, the big snub nose small in comparison with the bulk behind it and the scythe of its tail tall and proud and immense, sweeping far behind the head as if a sailfish were trailing the body and propelling it at a distance.

"Get in here, Harold," Cal yelled again and Harold, to Cal's amazement, began to sidestep, still staring at the shark that had turned to the south and seemed to be moving back along the surge line in their direction. Harold, for whatever reason, perhaps because the shark had taken him from his dreams and just at that moment, he remained poised between worlds, or perhaps because he'd suddenly awakened to his bravery and found himself at last to be redoubtable, a crowing beast, or, most likely, because he was utterly beside himself—Cal didn't care what it was—now shuffled not backward toward the lanai but sideways. Then, as Cal steadied the kayak in the channel between lava flows, Harold stumbled in, nearly upsetting it. He even grabbed the paddle from the floor, as though it were a sword, still straining his eyes out toward the sea.

•

Cal had never seen a tiger shark in the wild and supposed, to the extent he supposed at all, that Harold, who seemed fascinated with anything large, found the prospect of witnessing the animal up close too tempting to resist. It was certainly true that tigers rarely, almost never, approached such shallow coral embankments during the daylight hours. Occasionally there were sightings by open water swimmers along the shoreline north toward Kona and the odd attack on surfers, particularly when swells amped up and runoff from rains clouded coastal waters. But it remained an anomaly, something wild and mysterious, and Cal, for his part, did not hesitate to run for the kayak at the prospect of peering down at such power.

There was one other thing. Cal, who had dived with many sharks, had never been in the water with a tiger. They had a kind of mythical presence. When they did approach the shore it was usually at dusk and they had been known to surf, literally to surf, to use their wide bulks to navigate wave troughs, and fish along the break line when the sun had exited but still cast its gloaming rays. In other places, not Hawaii, Cal had sat on the beach and watched this happen. What had struck him then was not the danger of wading into the shallows but the need of such animals, the urgency that size brought to bear. There were stories of tigers slit open to reveal plough blades and tree branches and parts of cars.

Now he climbed in behind Harold to the seat at the stern and pushed off with his own paddle. They moved, incredibly, out toward the shark, as though they were one, as though the two of them had often, just before sunset, set off together in precisely this way, toward things you couldn't exactly envision from land but which, having lived them together in a kind of complicity and synchrony, they'd known for years and thrust into their knowledge of each other.

"That's it," purred Cal from behind, watching Harold work his paddle carefully, avoiding the outcroppings of jagged, coffee-colored lava. Then, "Now, good work," as they came to the surge zone elongated and rough with breaks arriving in three irregular rows across the flow banks. Here, to his amazement, Cal watched Harold dig in, bending his broad back toward the water and hauling powerfully with his arms, the big bulk of him at work, the head lifted up as though seeking something then the shoulders dipping back down to pull.

They were in a rhythm. It was maddening, thought Cal, to the extent that he was of a mind to think anything. Indeed, just at that moment he scarcely inhabited such a mind. He had almost no thinking in him at all except for a yearning for deep water, for the place he'd never brought Harold before where even from a kayak you could see depths, detect things displaced beneath other things, find animals passing beneath you and then, when you dove, gliding even above you, over you, between you and the air.

The shark was gone, so far as Cal could tell. Harold had stopped working his paddle and was sitting upright. The sun was blinding in the west and streaking through the surface of the sea into what was now a gorgeous blue, fine and clear at depth, marking out the place just ahead where the drop-off lay and beyond which other things, god knows what things, were alive and real, shooting into light you could scarcely see.

Out there, Cal knew, they would be beyond the tumult of the break line and the turbid brown water of the shallows, past even the green of the lava holes and, because it was already July, outside the coral bloom that began along the structures at the surface and persisted until the reef gave off, where the substrate of the ocean floor bent down into the gloom.

Cal had dived out there on many occasions, equalizing three times and passing down toward the curve in the coral floor where it arched to a sandy bottom below sixty feet in places and descended across outcroppings from there. From those outcroppings he would turn, his lungs pulled tight while the sun at that depth fell through curved shafts into a set of slung hammocks against the sand. Then he'd sail upward, thrusting with his ankles locked together. Finally, as he rose above fifty feet, the air would begin to boom inside him.

But that had not happened for a while. It had been some time since he'd been down there like that. Perhaps years. In fact, Cal could not recall when he'd last felt alive in a way he'd once taken for granted, testing his body, feeling it wrapped around his mind like cords of energy he could alternately tense and release, tap into. Harold too seemed tired, had been tired, Cal suspected, for perhaps fifteen years. He had been terribly affectionate when they'd first met. Too affectionate, if anything. Making it difficult to sleep. Indeed, Harold had been a wonderful lover, a great brute, a hurly-burly. And even now there were spurts of love, periods of grand warmth. But those too, if one thought it over, drew roots from an epoch of earthiness and treachery and reconfirmed belonging that had long passed. So at times it seemed to Cal as if they haunted separate spheres, as if for years he'd been walking slowly into the sea and the tide line was the breaking point where Harold left off and he began.

There was this, though—the impossibility of anything else was what you reached, what you earned. To Cal it seemed hardly conceivable that either of them at this late stage could ever renew or reset. Or be jolted. That too, he'd decided, was a kind of love, deep and trenching. And like the tide, it made grooves in you.

•

Now Cal could see Harold stiffen, the looseness in his limbs suddenly disappearing. Harold still held onto his paddle, but it was in one hand rather than across his thighs and the blade dragged into the water, slicing the surface insignificantly. He was shifted awkwardly in his seat, craning his neck.

"Gone," said Harold bemusedly, and Cal turned the kayak so they could see behind them, in the direction of the shore.

"I suppose so," he agreed, not wishing to disturb the fact that they had alit here silently as though atop a wide sky, that they'd settled in the water as if on spreading boughs that were invisible and belonged to nothing.

"Christ," blurted Harold suddenly, but Cal was not sure why.

Now they both stared outward and to the west, squinting, and were motionless. The wind was already coming down, eddying elsewhere, stirring beyond the bay somewhere in the offing before it would stiffen again just as they lay back to sleep in the small bed beside tall screened windows that faced the sea.

Cal dipped his paddle and shoved them forward, farther from

shore, watching Harold who was still swiveling, scanning the surface and looking downward into water at last clear and deep.

When the shark came it was from behind and beneath them, rising and sweeping under the kayak from the back. Its bulk was perhaps a yard under their feet at its closest, the dorsal fin alone filling much of that space. It was just to the starboard, coming below their right hands and passing massively, for a long time, the snout abrupt, then the black intelligent eye, gills vulnerable and white on their ruffling insides, and the skin mottled by huge, broken swatches of dun. The upper lobe of the tail was what moved, long and smooth like a sail.

Cal could not see the look on Harold's face. He had not thought of Harold in the moment it took for the shark to pass. He himself was elated, as though a soft electric current had swept through him, had coursed through his insides, and he wanted to touch Harold, to make sure he too had felt this thing, this immensity.

"Fifteen, maybe sixteen feet," he shouted to Harold. But Harold was already falling. Having twisted around in his seat, his hands to his right along the thin rim of the kayak shell that lacked the deep gunnel of a dinghy, Harold had jerked himself forward to see the broad swath of the tail glide beneath him. Now, for an instant, he was curved sideways, grappling to regain his balance, hips hulked dangerously out away from his shoulders and left hand shooting to grab his seat. It was too late. Harold's bulk took him right, nearly overturning the kayak. Harold himself plunged into the sea, his shoulder in first then his jowls and head then the heavy rest of him, all of it disappearing for a moment before the pale back of the neck showed and he was bobbing at the surface, hallooing and monstrous, pouncing for the kayak as though there were something below him to leap from, tossing out his arms and letting them flop into the hollow below his seat before he was sinking back down again, returning to the ocean with his great throat sputtering and eyes in the waves.

Cal could see a moment of horror in Harold's face that held all moments. This, after all, was why you swam in the sea—the thought flashed in Cal's mind—so there was an element of readiness about you. As Harold had no experience of sharks, his legs, Cal imagined, would feel like blooded meat, seeping even before their butchery, and he, Harold, must sense them now hung languidly down for slaughter.

"Harold—reach out and take your paddle," yelled Cal. Unlike other pairs who'd invented bedroom names or other flip endearments, he and Harold through a kind of tacit formality and his own inveterate shyness had never taken such license. Now Cal leaned forward but could not quite reach Harold's paddle bumping on the surface of the blue ocean away from them.

"Swim out and grab your paddle, Harold." But it was like talking to a fool. Harold was clamoring madly, stabbing for a hold of his seat in the kayak with both hands and pulling the rim violently to the starboard.

Cal leaned left to balance him and began to crawl toward the bow in an attempt to gain a purchase on Harold's broad shoulders and heave him back aboard. But before he'd gone far, he realized he would not have the strength to lift a man as big as Harold, and Harold, he knew, would soon spend himself in his panic and turn listless and deadweighted. For now, the kayak wobbled dangerously as Harold flailed and vainly sought a handhold, an oarlock, at last a gunwale that was not there.

“Stop splashing,” shouted Cal. “It will attract the shark.”

And Harold ceased, already exhausted, his eyes bright and strange, contaminated with fright in a way that Cal had not witnessed in anyone, that did not fit with what he’d known. Initially he’d thought to drag Harold beside the boat, to paddle him into the safety of the reef structures. But now he changed course.

“I’m going to flip it,” he hollered. And Cal grabbed hold of the right rim of the kayak and shifted his weight to the left, letting himself splash down into the ocean on the far side of Harold and pulling the kayak with him until it was inverted. He guessed that the shark would be near, that there had been too much commotion for it not to circle and return, so he dove down several feet beneath the tide wash and gazed out scanning into the water, his vision maskless and bleary, before he lifted his head to surface.

•

“Now we’ll get on together,” Cal said more quietly, “at the same time,” trying to reach Harold with his eyes, Harold whom he could not see, as the broad yellow plastic of the kayak, built for tourists and novices, rounded out above the level of his vision. He weighted the back end and, to his surprise, there was Harold on the far side at the front, coughing and pulling himself up onto the inverted bow until the two of them were lying awkwardly in a line, facing the western horizon and the deep sea, their legs straddling the plastic and splayed out, chests full on the kayak bottom, and the whole enterprise sunk a foot, or a foot and a half, below the rocking surface of the waves.

Cal saw that Harold had a paddle wedged beneath his armpit. He, Cal, had lost his own paddle, not thinking to grab it before he’d turned the kayak, and he cursed himself now for this omission. But Harold must have found it. Somehow, it must have floated to him. In any case, Harold had a grip on the paddle now, had shifted it into his right hand and, to Cal looking across Harold's back toward the crown of his head, his partner seemed suddenly armed, as though he were preparing for something, girding for battle.

"If it comes to it, go for the butt of the snout and the eyes," Cal hissed. "If you can manage it, jab at the face, strike him above the mouth."

But Harold looked to be concentrating on the water just in front of him, fixated on something that Cal, from his vantage, couldn't quite make out.

"Stay close to the boat whatever happens," Cal went on. "We make a larger shape together."

Perhaps thirty seconds or another minute slipped by like this, with them lying on their chests, grasping the overturned kayak as though they were riding a wobbling missile through the air, their bodies largely submerged, the water covering their backs, and their heads moving on a swivel, eyes on both men scanning. Their feet and even knees hung more deeply in the sea on one side of the kayak or the other, then pulled up hastily, then dropped down again for balance.

"Stay quiet with your legs if he comes. Lift them out and shift them away from him."

But Harold gave no indication, had given no indication, that he could hear Cal speaking from behind him in the stillness. He remained fixated on the water in front of the kayak, as though spinner dolphins were circling in the brilliant blue beneath them. Cal remembered that spinners and tigers were famously ill-disposed to one another, that they were enemies. He thought perhaps in the winter they would laugh about all of this, the two of them holding one another on the beach like they had done regularly in those first years after his inheritance, basking in their good fortune. Harold, who was always more voluble in company, whom Cal would watch shyly and admire, would tell the neighbors the outrageous story of their humping a kayak and he, Cal, would search out pieces of olivine in the sand and pile them on Harold's stomach while it rumbled and shook as he came to the part about dolphins. Perhaps, he thought, there were spinners beneath them now.

As the shark rose, its dorsal slit the surface evenly, sixty feet in front of them, without the conspicuous swivel that would suggest aggression. However, he was moving on them directly, in a line. Cal could see the large scythe of the tail working well behind the dorsal and breaking the surface at intervals to either side of the body. The sun was in their eyes as the shark came in and what they could glimpse was limited by the glare. Though Cal could not make out the head just yet, he knew where it was in the water.

"Coming," he whispered to Harold. "Stay steady."

The shark left its course and built a slow circle, perhaps fifteen feet in radius. Cal could clearly see the eye that was round and jet black and seemed to stare at him directly as the shark made its first pass to his port side. It was a magnificent eye, old and patient. Then it was behind him and though the shark finished its circle and completed one more, Cal did not see the eye again but was caught instead by the ravaged field of skin, by opalescent scars ripped above the mouth and tattering the left ventral fin. The breadth of the fish in its middle was wide as his Toyota. Tiger swatches, faded and worn, made the shark's sides pass on and on, becoming shapeless, decorated walls that narrowed only after a long time to the tail.

When Cal watched the shark veer after its two circles and start to swing its tail wide, he barked, "No," but by then it was already in on Harold with its body arched upward and the head lifted nearly out of the water and Harold was falling backward and off to the left, the whole bow of the kayak momentarily jerked down from great weight and Cal himself raised up, grasping for the plastic as he came off into the sea then clumsily stroking for the stern and hauling himself back on before finally, reinstalled and safe, searching wildly for Harold who had disappeared.

•

Reports of attacks in Hawaiian waters that had circulated over the years in which Cal had followed them tended to highlight the same things. There was generally surf involved, one way or another, and victims tended not to be diving but stretched upon the surface or occasionally wading to the shoulders. Spear fisherman reported encounters but mostly with smaller sharks like blues and oceanic whitetips that could be dangerous but rarely attacked divers. The tiger, on the other hand, was famously unpredictable. It was the foremost attack species in the Hawaiian archipelago. Most of the time it would circle and depart but if there was activity or fear it could remain, become aggressive. The key was to stay calm, not turn your back, and so long as your eyes were in the water, drop both legs together to show your length. In any case, Cal had purposefully skimmed over the rare articles pronouncing incidents on grounds that, in the event of a sighting, he would be in a kayak or well beneath the surface and Harold, in all likelihood, would be watching from the safety of the shore.

Now a kind of fuzz occupied segments of Cal's vision, toward the peripheries, and a loud stillness sat in his ears as if the ocean had been amplified to the point where he ceased to hear it. He saw the shark surface to his right, perhaps thirty feet off. Seconds elapsed which he initially failed to register but which then filtered back as a vague gap in time. Harold, who somehow had been swept far left of Cal and slightly to his rear, emerged, surfacing loudly, still grasping the paddle and sputtering. In another moment he was performing the crawl, majestically and, for all that Cal could discern, steadily and calmly with the paddle crashing on the surface at the stroke of his right arm.

Yet inexplicably he was swimming outward, toward the depths, in the direction of the blue ocean. Cal hoisted himself forward to the center of the overturned kayak and called out to Harold in order to offer him direction. But, again, it was as though one or both of them could no longer hear, or as if the force of events had not only clogged Harold's ears but in so doing made off with his mind.

"Harold," Cal yelled, "over here." But it was for naught. To his horror, Cal watched as the shark swam toward the kayak and submerged, sinking its bulk only just under, so he could nearly reach down and touch those irregular bands and follow the shadowy markings with his thumb. It continued beneath him, still submerged, toward Harold who, bizarrely, horribly, was swimming out to sea in a beautiful noisy crawl. Now he was pointed toward Maui and the deepening trench, moving like a great slow van of milkshakes and sugar cones that was ringing all its bells.

"Harold," Cal yelled again. "Shark!"

Now, as though this last word stirred something, awakened him, Harold lifted his head and peered in the direction of the voice then sharply shifted course, his rough beard suddenly visible in the waves, his eyes heavily lidded at first, then wide open. He began swimming toward the tiger shark, and toward Cal, wielding the paddle out before him in awkward half strokes like a ridiculous spear. Then, without slowing his kick that was shooting fountains behind him, Harold began jousting with his weapon, raising it absurdly and slapping the sea in front of him, spearing the space between him and the shark. If anything, it looked to Cal, lying motionless on the kayak, as though Harold was picking up speed and at last he was bellowing, making a noise that was unidentifiable but deep and final.

As the two of them converged, Cal could see the tall dorsal fin of the tiger shark that had been swerving on the surface rise mightily into the air and Harold begin to sink, as though he were cowering before a blow.

"No," yelled Cal once again, slapping his own arm impotently against the ocean and nearly losing his balance.

But just before contact, Harold reappeared. Having lowered himself, he raised his whole chest out of the water, or nearly, and once reared, brought the paddle, blade first, down like a javelin with what looked to Cal like tremendous force. There was a jerk and Harold was brought sharply into the air while the tiger flashed its tail and rolled seaward, turning abruptly, the dorsal sinking off and away.

Cal, meanwhile, watched in amazement as Harold, after vanishing again for what felt like ten seconds or more, surfaced twenty feet off, again farther to the left and closer to the safety of the lava flows. After briefly wiping his eyes, he resumed his slow recreational crawl, his giant fountain kick, this time shoreward, the handle of the paddle still in his hand, the blade and much of the shaft now broken off and missing. Every so often, Harold would pause as he proceeded toward the lava and turn, dipping his head beneath the surface as if to gaze into the depths behind him, then lifting his eyes to scan the horizon. In these moments, he would raise the jagged shaft of the paddle and wield it threateningly and, having waited for an instant, turn back to the grand strokes of his crawl.

Finally, Harold stood in the shallows and was yelling out to him, "Stay where you are. Don't move. I'm coming with the dinghy." In another few minutes, there was Harold, having dragged the dinghy down to the shore from behind the house, the mynah birds quarreling over him in the jacaranda or swooping onto the sand to swagger like field generals at his feet. Then he was rowing swiftly through the lava breaks. A few minutes more and Cal found himself being helped onto the dinghy, Harold's strong arms pulling him up over the gunwale and placing him gently onto the dry seat.

"Thank you, Harold," said Cal, gathering himself and watching as Harold turned back to the oars, taking his sweet time now, his arms from that angle appearing particularly round and wide, pulling the two of them in to safety with long powerful leisurely strokes.

•

When they reached the shore, Harold beached the dinghy and they stood together, quiet, the two of them staring for a short time out toward the sea and shifting their bare feet on the lava. Cal could just see the rocking hull of the kayak, largely submerged, humped like the yellow rind of a melon.

"Tiger's a brutal fish," he sputtered at last, shaking his head. "He'll kill you in an instant." And he felt his whole body quivering, as though a wildness had corded his limbs until then and only now, in a single moment, swung them back to his frame. Cal realized for the first time he could recall that he'd been fighting to hold himself upright. He decided, moreover, if he did not monitor his breaths and broaden his stance he would need to lean on Harold, or at least take him by the shoulder. Finally, so as not to fall over, he squatted down.

There was another long pause while the sun began to falter. The remaining light was slung low and sharp. A breeze had come up.

"Now everything has a belly," said Harold softly, his voice even and serious. He placed his big paws on his own belly that was beautiful, grand, and drumlike, and began to chuckle so softly that Cal could scarcely hear him. Then Cal also began to laugh, glancing up at his lover, staring at him with a curious intensity, a kind of fascination, each of them coming to the other's eyes, and for a moment they were laughing together before Harold was moving up the beach, looking every so often back at the ocean then swinging his grand neck forward toward the spreading shade of the house.

"Harold," Cal called after him, but the sound got stuck in his throat. He watched that hulking form, still wet and scraped badly along one side of its ribs, the bright line of abrasion curving back almost to the spine. It climbed surely, effortlessly, up onto the lanai as if it had only just stepped out from the froth of the waves, barnacled and metamorphosed.

"Harold, wait."

Yet again he was voiceless, silent. Soon Cal was stumbling into the sand. Trying to keep up. Struggling to move closer to the house and farther onto land. Exhausted, he hung there out on the beach attempting to master himself but, as the pure soot of darkness rolled in from the sea, he dropped first to his haunches and then to his knees.

ONE ROAD

It was late and he'd had a few beers when the truck rolled on him, and he ended up nearly upside down with the wheels hung in the air. It was a big rig for such a road. And he was a little drunk. The truth was he'd been making up time after the river crossing and the long dinner he'd had at the rest house on the north bank of the Essequibo River, and now he'd come around a bend too quickly. For a long while, uninjured, Michael lay in the cab across the backrest of the passenger seat, his feet drawn forward to lie poised upon the windshield. His lights were still on. In fact, the vehicle was still engaged in gear. But he was going nowhere.

The forest loomed closely on both sides. His engine had caught and shut off as the truck bellied over, and now the noise of the forest grew loud and insistent. The cry of the screaming piha, high in the overhanging canopy, began as a low whistle that got louder until it came in bursts at the end of each call. It was an astounding sound, one they tried to imitate in the mines. Some of the miners, from Brazil, from Boa Vista and farther to the south, had perfected it. They could arouse an entire tract of forest. Even so, the bauxite mines, having begun in the northeast corner of Guyana, along the Berbice River, had spread their operations. Now small-time gold mining had proliferated. In places along riverbanks where land dredges and mechanized sluices had been set up, first the animals then even the birds had fled. The men, hungry and bored, would hunt out the capybara and the peccary and even shoot at harpy eagles if they found their roosts. Soon, after only two weeks on-site, in many places you could make your call and nothing would answer.

But not here. Along the road you could still see anything, at any time, and the screaming pihas, though nearly invisible, were loud and abundant in the canopy. Michael rose and felt his back which seemed fine, surprisingly intact. He climbed out of the passenger-side window, the plexiglass long gone after so many years, up onto the side of the truck that now faced upper branches and the sky. He climbed out onto the tire then hung down and dropped. He was strong and athletic. While the other men were often fighters at the mines, he was not. He could take punishment though. He prided himself on that. He had never started a fight in his life. But he'd lived through many.

The last pontoon ferry at Kurupukari had been at six p.m. He'd made it north in time for that, coming up from Lethem with full cargo, and then, after the fish and beers, there were several hours of driving in the dark without another vehicle the whole stretch. Then this. The bend in the dirt track had come just after a rise and he'd accelerated to make the grade. Now he was sunk in a low valley, where the track had been converted by recent rains into deep mud sloughs, and he walked beside the truck in bare feet through standing water up to his thighs.

Nonetheless, it was warm. Even beforehand, he'd been sweating in the cab, negotiating long, deep potholes and getting out here and there in the night to drag a heavy tree limb out of the road. Michael thought to try his cell phone which he still had on him, despite everything. He'd had service ten hours south in Lethem but now, in the deep forest, there was no connectivity. He calculated he was still roughly five hours short of Georgetown. Best to wait it out. By no means could he leave his rig. It was chock-full of a hodgepodge of things: a quarter shipment of orange juice in waxed paper containers from Bonfim across the Takutu River in Brazil; suction hoses that were in need of repair before they went up for sale; sluice boxes, light blue and immovable; and other gear from the mines that went back and forth from Lethem to Georgetown on the Caribbean Sea.

Michael dared not climb back into the cab. The overturned truck lay half in and half out of the deep mud track of the road and anything coming from either direction would need to brake sharply on soft loam to avoid colliding with it. He had no flares or cones, but he waded and then trudged up the near side of the valley, from which he'd come, and stationed himself there. From the north, he reasoned, vehicles would have slightly more time to stop or evade. From this side, on the other hand, he could give them warning himself.

After a dark chunk of night, several hours, a vehicle did come. Standing on the rise, he could only hear it at first. Then he glimpsed lights flickering and disappearing as the vehicle dipped into the long, deep holes on the track. Finally, it had climbed the hill and Michael hailed it, waving his arms and standing in the center of the road. It was a Toyota Hilux. He could see that by the lights and the roof of the single cab. He noted as it drew near there was a woman in the cab and an elderly driver, an African, gray-haired and spare, perhaps feeble. The woman was white, relatively young, and she looked frightened, wary at the least.

"I've overturned," shouted Michael into the open windows, sticking his head into the vehicle and staring first at the driver and then at the woman in the back who was upright and alert, lit softly in red by the vehicle's faint interior glow. "You won't pass tonight."

The old man at the wheel gazed down away from Michael into the slim valley at the truck on its side. When Michael turned his own head there was almost nothing else beyond the truck. A pitch blackness reigned down there. The forest canopy foreshortened the view and narrowed it to a tunnel, while the beams of the Hilux caught his sideways rig aslant so the canvas tie-down over the long truck bed threw up a gray, steaming mass of light.

"Well, there must be a way around," said the woman from the back seat.

"Not tonight," answered Michael. "They'll need a full excavator, probably a fuel truck, and a work team from Linden." He groaned inwardly. It had never happened before to him, though he'd seen it a hundred times on the road. What was worse for the other vehicles trying to pass was that it was not a company truck. It was his own. He'd bought it in Bonfim and begun a kind of transit business three years earlier to escape the malaria that was sweeping the small-time gold concessions. The mines deep in the Guyanese forest were populated with workers from Brazil coming in by sea to Rio de Janeiro from Pakistan and the Philippines, and the foremen were mostly Creoles who spoke Portuguese. Michael was from Georgetown on the northern coast, his mother from Trinidad, and the rainforest famously spelled sickness, bred by sheer numbers of transients and poor conditions for those who came down into the interior from the capital to work in the gold and bauxite mines to the south. In any case, the truck was his, and there was no company to dispatch its men down from Linden into the interior to help gather his cargo from the mud and haul out the vehicle in the event it was no longer roadworthy. So they would have to wait for the work crews.

"No phone," whispered the driver, "or I'd give it to you."

Michael looked at the old man and smiled.

"It's all right, father," he said. "We'll get by."

"What do you mean not tonight?" asked the woman after an extended pause.

"One road," answered Michael. "And it's blocked."

•

Michael looked at the woman in the back seat of the vehicle. For some reason, she was scarcely visible now. A voice with the dimmest of bodies. He waited for her to speak again. If for no other reason, then the better to locate her.

"How long?" she asked.

Michael thought for a moment. It was already late, perhaps one in the morning.

"By the afternoon."

He heard her sigh. "That's too late."

It turned out the woman had a plane to catch in Georgetown. Once she finally stepped out of the Hilux, as though reconciled at last to the possibility of delay, she began to speak freely, liberally, about all kinds of things. She was surprisingly open. Even trusting, Michael thought.

"There's another way around," he told her after a while. "But it's not a road."

The woman perked up, seemed interested, so he continued.

"It's a hunter's trail. You'd have to walk."

"From here? Where will I get by walking from here?"

Indeed, they were over a hundred kilometers south of Linden and the Demerara River, then another hundred to Georgetown.

"Not far," croaked the old driver. "You won't get far."

"You'll get to a local village." And the woman looked at Michael, her eyes coming over to his across the forest. She was staring at him now, measuring him maybe. She had come out into the headlights and was startlingly tall and slender.

"Where's that?" she asked quietly.

"It's an Amerindian village. Macushi people," Michael explained. And she was silent.

"You can get transport from there. There'll be a truck. They've cut a track back to the road."

The old man still had the engine running, because he's an old man, thought Michael, and now he's lost his sense.

"Save your gas," whispered Michael to the driver, and the old man shut off his engine. It hissed and died. Almost immediately, it seemed, the driver had been swallowed by the coming day of motionlessness. He'd slumped down in his seat. He was preparing to sleep. Apparently pretending to think through options to help the woman, but already falling asleep. By then, in any case, she had stepped back into the darkness.

"If your driver stays with my rig, I can take you."

Michael thought he'd salvage something that way. Maybe she'd pay him. And he could place some calls once they had made it in the truck from the village out to the next gas depot. There at the depot, fifty kilometers north along the road, there was a phone, and he could eat lunch and alert his buyers to the prospect of delay.

"In the dark?" the woman asked.

“I’ve got a light,” answered Michael, “and I know the route.”

He could not see if the woman was looking at him doubtfully or with interest. The forest cloaked her, reached forward to cover her body, and shut out all but a narrow stripe of the sky. She was blonde. Her hair long and tied back neatly. But these were things he’d noted with some uncertainty before, first in the red glow of the Hilux and then again in the wash of its beams. Now he could see almost nothing. It was again a matter of her voice, of waiting to hear if it would speak again. And what it would say.

“So where is this path, and how long?”

It turned out she had an air of authority about her. She was important, experienced, Michael thought. He’d lived in America for seven years, just north of Miami, with an uncle who ran a cargo business. It was an import/export firm and Michael had given it seven years of his blood. Traveling all over the Caribbean, to Guatemala and Honduras, and back and forth to Caracas with shipping containers of kidney beans and coffee. Businesspeople all over the world were the same, he thought.

“Up ahead. Maybe five kilometers north. Then two hours in the forest.”

“Why not just walk the road until it hits their truck track—and follow *that* into the village?”

Michael began to believe she was intelligent, perhaps too intelligent either to trust or to fool, though he wasn’t granting anything yet.

“I think I’ll wait,” she told the driver who had already closed his eyes and nodded off, his mouth spread open.

And she drifted away, as though the two of them, she and Michael, had never been speaking. As though she and her driver, after the long slog together through the mud sloughs and the water holes and the screaming pihas, were still out on the road alone.

•

The mercury they used to break down the soil substratum before suctioning out the gold would leach into stagnant pools created by mechanized sluices around the mines. Most of these mines were illegal and brought by the road. With the road came access, and when it first crossed the Demerara River at Linden in 1968, the old cattle trail all the way into the interior to Annai became a dirt track navigable by mechanized vehicles into the heart of the forest and down into sprawling savannah country. The illegal mines that sprang up now by the day were often far south, destroying rich habitats where Wapishana and Wai-wai peoples fished and hunted, and while the stagnant pools within the streambeds brought hordes of mosquitoes and malaria to crowded workers, the mercury and the noise forced animal migrations and created temporary dead zones in the heart of the rainforest.

One result was that Amerindian villagers traveled farther into the forest for food. Hunters made longer trips, were gone for greater periods, and took higher risks to find sustenance. Some of them did not come back. A few lost their way. Others were killed or waylaid by temporary workers from Brazil who were frequently bitter or concealing illegal operations. There were feuds in the forest over land, over mine slurry and tailings that were bad for hunting and killed the fish. But not a few of these Macushi and Wapishana men who walked deep into the forest in search of bush pig and bush cow were killed by *Lachesis*, or the bushmaster, whom they called a silent bringer of death.

“That truck track is not safe for walking,” Michael explained softly to the woman, so as not to wake the driver, after almost a half an hour had gone by. “There can be snakes.”

He had approached her warily, to explain himself. She was lying in the back of the Hilux and he pushed his face only a small distance in through the open window toward her feet. She was sprawled out lengthwise on the seats.

“It is safer to walk the other way if you would like to walk.” He waited for her to speak then added, “Along the hunter’s trail.”

“I think I’ll wait,” she repeated.

Strangely, however, after several more minutes when he’d resumed his post on the road, Michael heard the door of the Hilux creak open and gently close, and she came out to him. She must have been thinking it over after all.

“You have a light?” she asked.

“Yes, I have a good light.”

“Well, I have headlamps and batteries,” and she pointed toward the Hilux.

“Bring them if you’d like to go, but they will be too small.” Michael got up and walked down into the low valley then waded into the cold water to where his rig lay. He climbed up the front grill then over to the window and located behind the passenger seat his handheld flashlight, which was a large, industrial LED.

“What kind of snakes?” she asked when he was back on the rise and squatting beside her. She’d sat down on the sideboard that was bent and pulling off the chassis of the Hilux, and her knees came up high.

“Bushmasters.”

And once again she was talking freely. She explained she had been hiking with a group and they'd run into trouble in the Iwokrama Rainforest farther to the south. Conservation land that, apart from official census gridding and an occasional scientific transect, mainly for poison dart frogs or butterflies, was scarcely explored. They'd seen no pit vipers, but a woman in their party broke her leg on a river crossing beyond the Iwokrama Range, on the far side of the mountains from the road. The rivers were swollen from heavy rains and chock-full of boulders. Two local Amerindian men had built a body sling out of cecropia branches and a hammock and they and the four foreigners, alternating portage, had all made it out but it took them five days. Now she'd had to hire this ancient fossil and his Hilux, and even so she was likely to miss her flight. There were other things too. Promises to a friend. A surgery. But from what Michael could make out, the woman herself was not ill. The surgery was for someone else.

"That's a good truck you're in," Michael said simply after all of it. "An old Hilux like this—they're stronger than trucks they make today." He paused, splaying out his hands on the hood and leaving them, weighted. "It'll get you there."

•

But the woman decided she couldn't wait after all. So Michael walked over to the driver and cupped the small, bony shoulder. He shook him gently. The man murmured in his sleep but was far away. When Michael shook him again, more vigorously, he awoke and shot his eyes into Michael's through the dimness, then flinched.

"It's all, right, father," Michael purred. "I need you to watch my rig."

He arranged it all with the driver. If, when Michael had returned and they'd cleared a lane around his rig, the old man would give him a lift to Georgetown, Michael would pay for his gas then hire the old man to drive him back into the interior to the crash site. There would be no difference in the pay, he assured him. The driver would get the money that was coming to him.

Then he showed the woman his light.

"That is strong," she agreed.

In the meantime, she'd shouldered her pack, which was large. When Michael offered to carry it for her, she refused him. She was strong, he noticed. Tall and strong. And, since the old man had dropped off again into his dreams, they walked down the road toward the quagmire.

After they'd passed his rig and waded through the high water and out of the mud they started up the far slope and legged out several kilometers on the road. Still nothing came. There were no vehicles out here in the middle of the night. People waited for dawn to head into the interior unless they were desperate or late.

The truth was it had been years since the last time Michael had been out through the forest to this Macushi village. At least ten years earlier, he'd hiked out for a wage on behalf of a speculator from the capital who sought to initiate a timber operation without the permits. The villagers had said no. The man had ready money to offer up front, he'd explained, and, after all, they had done the work to build the truck track. But the villagers hadn't so much as deliberated. Secretly, he'd been relieved. Several times afterward, he had walked the hunter's path before he owned a vehicle to renew the man's offer. Each time, they had invited him to spend the night. They'd fed him generously. They hadn't laughed or mistreated or threatened him. They hadn't murdered him in his bed. They had even warned him about the danger of the truck track, about the threat of bushmaster along that track. And always he'd felt like a dog, a black dog from the capital, and ridden in the bed of their vehicle back out to the road.

"Why should I trust you?" asked the woman when they were still walking on the road and there was no moon and there were already kilometers opened up between them and the Hilux and the sleeping old man.

But Michael ignored the question. Instead, he told her about the problem with the truck track from the road out to the village—it was rough and narrow and consisted in two tire grooves in the red mud with heavy vegetation in the center that scraped the undercarriage and grew up above hood level of a pickup.

"The bushmaster hides in the center of the track," he told her soberly. "In the brush."

"What for?"

"Anything that comes."

They never found the forest path. Finding forest paths off the road on a moonless night was one of those things everyone believed they could do but almost no one could. Even with a good light. Once in a while maybe, when you were fortunate. But few carried that kind of fortune inside them.

"We must have passed it," Michael said at last. He expected the woman to be full of blame. To turn against him. But she was silent.

"Should we turn back and search?" she asked after they'd continued to walk.

"I don't know. It may have grown over. They may not use it much now."

He imagined she was considering. Turning it all over in her head as usual. That soon she would suggest what he himself was bound to suggest: that they were better off turning back.

But since she said nothing, they continued walking for reasons Michael did not fully understand, with the canopy arched over the road and leering. With the screaming pihas perched invisibly above like high-pitched telephones searching for signals, seeking a bead on something far away and receding.

For several hours, they walked on until, according to Michael's estimates, they were beginning to approach the truck track to the village that left the road and wandered into the forest for six kilometers or so. Once, along the way, a vehicle passed. They hailed it in order to warn the driver of the downed rig. But it was on the downslope of the hill, just after it had crested a rise, and it careened past them, radio blaring.

"He must have seen us waving," said the woman.

"Yes," said Michael. "They don't always stop. Sometimes, there are bad people out on the road at night."

The woman appeared to shrug this off. She was tireless. Michael himself carried only his truck keys and the heavy flashlight. He had a hunting knife strapped to the side of his leg between calf and shin, sheathed all in leather. Yet other than that he was walking freely. The woman, on the other hand, was burdened. Her pack must have weighed seventy-five kilos, based on the way she'd loaded up, and it was bulging full. Yet she strode onward now, straight through the mud sloughs, lifting her feet powerfully, wading up to her waist in places, but moving quickly and without hesitation.

Finally, when they came to the break in the forest edge that held Michael's step, she halted with him and waited.

He shined the light, arced it across the track, pausing at each of the truck grooves then sketching the line of the canopy above.

"This is the truck track," he said finally. "We can wait here and perhaps they will drive out after dawn."

"And what if they don't?"

"Then we can catch a ride back to your driver and wait."

Once again, the woman seemed to be mulling her options. "This goes straight to the village?"

"Yes."

"Then if I can walk with your light, I think I'll take the risk."

"No," said Michael. "Here it's not safe to walk." And he moved over toward her and barred her way.

Yet immediately she stepped around him. In a kind of blur. It was still a ways short of dawn. Maybe an hour. Michael had glimpsed stars directly overhead in the darkness that, if anything, had been intensifying over the course of their swift progress on the road.

"I'm sorry," she said very loudly, and then, as she'd done earlier in the night, repeated herself more firmly. "But I think I'll take the risk."

Michael watched as the woman moved onto the truck track. He watched until she was no longer a form but only her own dim light. In the meantime, he called out to her to stop. He yelled to her. He hollered into the darkness toward her meager headlamp that in certain years, he'd been told, the track had served as a breeding site. That you could not predict when. That the worst time though was at night. He yelled everything they'd told him ten years earlier as the headlamp flickered out in front, grew distant.

Then Michael cursed and unsheathed his long, straight knife and for no reason he could follow, because he was suddenly in league with all the insanity of his life, tore off down the truck track into the dark forest with the knife stretched crosswise, blade outward, in front of his throat.

•

When he found the woman, she was already on the ground. He rushed toward her, brandishing his knife, flashing the area with his light. Preparing to defend her. But she was beginning to rise.

"I just stumbled. I'm fine."

She lifted herself in one motion as he watched, pivoting as he did so to turn his light into the understory. Then she was back on her feet and moving.

"Please at least wear your pack in the front."

She paused and he waited as she removed her pack and repositioned the harness.

"And please let me walk in front with my light."

Michael could feel that he was tired, beyond tired. It had been a long time since the fish and beers and the last light on the surface of the river. The woman said nothing, but she slowed down and allowed him to lead her. He noted that she walked in the same tire track, behind him, and did not complain of his pace. As he scoured the vegetation at the center of the track, and poked his light among fallen limbs, across lianas, into the crannies of buttressed roots, he began mildly to relax. After a short while, once again, she began talking. She was a doctor. She carried antivenin wherever she went. She'd spent years in what she called "the tropics," which was a term Michael seldom heard in Guyana. Before long, in an endless, rapid train of words, she was saying things like "knowledge transfer" and "indigenous community" and "sustainable practices" and "bioprospecting."

"The bushmaster," he told her by way of reply, "will coil in one place for two weeks. If you see him before he can strike, and turn back the other way, he will wait for many days, hoping you return."

"But why would it do that?" asked the woman.

"We don't know," said Michael. "Because he is angry."

Then Michael explained that many men when they were clearing for a mine were killed by bushmasters. That his father, again and again, had warned him a bushmaster, with his broad head, his heavy body, with the tall ridge on his back and his long-folded fangs, has the gift of being small and silent right up until the moment when he stands up.

"He waits there quietly in the dark until, before you see him, he is already a tower, striking at your chest or your head. If he can, he will hit your eyes."

The woman seemed unfazed. She said very little about this threat, as if the snake was of no concern.

"Yes," she said, "they are two, maybe three meters long and very wide in the body. The venom is hemotoxic. So, organ degeneration. But I'm told you rarely see them."

Toward dawn, an agouti scurried across their path, a noisy, furred rodent ball, gorged on Brazil nuts.

"Only agouti," said Michael, and at last, as the light was growing, slanting through the trees, they reached the village. There was a truck there. Michael began to make inquiries, but soon the woman was speaking on her own behalf. He fell silent. When she mentioned the bushmaster and the truck track, one of the older men laughed.

"Nothing like that anymore. Too, too many trucks," and he laughed again. The woman laughed also, but quietly, not unkindly, Michael thought. She seemed relieved to have found transport.

There was a light in her voice. Something serious must be calling her home, he decided. When the topic of the danger of snakes came up a second time, they were already making arrangements to depart. Again, there was laughter. This time, a group of villagers loitering by the truck began speaking of the bushmaster, of how he could stay silent and survive by eating only ten times in a year. But one of those times, they said, it must be a brocket deer or a man, or he will starve. Michael spoke up in earnest then for the first time since their arrival. He said more than once at the mines they'd seen two bites come from a single strike, one on the neck and one just above. And although he did not, the villagers around him laughed very hard at this. Pointing their eyes politely toward the ground when he remained serious.

"No, no," said one of the Macushi men, grinning, who was dressed in ragged overalls, who had a wrench in his hand and was preparing the truck. Who now, after whatever he had done in the past, was the driver of a truck to Georgetown? "The bushmaster has gone far into the forest." He waved his hand in the air away from the road, then let it drop soundlessly to his side.

"Too many trucks," repeated another, shaking his head, and the woman smiled at Michael and offered again to take him first to his rig before they headed north to the capital.

"No," he assured her, "you're late. I will walk on the hunter's path back to the road."

She looked at him seriously.

"I'd feel better if you came with us," she said, this new, bright voice in her, as though she were two people. Even her eyes, for the first time, now the light was in the sky, were stalling over his eyes. "After everything you've done."

But Michael no longer cared to move forward with his plan. In fact, he felt strongly that he would not like to take payment from this woman. Something somewhere, perhaps when she'd plowed past him, despite his warnings, onto the truck track, or when the villagers had laughed into the ground, had filled him with disgust. For the first time since she'd arrived, glowing in the red light of the Hilux, seated behind the bent old man, he harbored no curiosity whatsoever. He did not want to know what it was she was rushing toward, or comprehend the nature of her projects, or witness her exhilaration, the gratitude she felt, having had her adventure and now, with his aid, orchestrated an escape.

"Come," she said, confidingly, stepping toward him, as if they'd traveled together for months and faced perils they alone were aware of. As if they had saved each other. And he felt suddenly as if he had known this foreign woman his whole life, as if he had been escorting someone who was busy and more important and even beautiful for as long as he could remember. Though he'd scarcely spoken except in reply, and he had never told her his name.

•

As he walked back to his rig and the sleeping old man along the narrow forest trail without having made his calls to clients, without ever reaching the gas depot, he was thinking soon there would be many roads into the interior. And soon there would be many drivers like him. But now, when there was just one road, it was still possible to see a jaguar drying its pelage after the noon rains. She would come out, the jaguar, into a patch of sun pooling brightly on the road where the canopy broke above her. Toucans were often perched at these forest breaks, silhouetted like half-broken branches. Everything had nearly changed, but not yet.

Now Michael moved with caution on the hunter's path that was once the old cattle trail to Annai but was badly overgrown. Despite everything that was said, and despite the laughter that rang in his ears, he instinctively looked to the sides and far ahead. He used what little sunlight penetrated so far, slanting sharply from the east past epiphytes and bromeliads, through the understory of the forest. And in the instant he saw the snake, the blood rushing inside him, he stepped back then stepped back again, slowly, a longer step, so he was just far enough to marvel at its size, at the rough scales on the telltale dorsal ridge, the broad, flattened triangle head, at its height which came even with his ribs. To return the gaze of this giant, this killer so close and alive, hiding only a few kilometers from the village and the road, and witness its quiet beauty.

For a moment, he stood there breathing, those sheened eyes staring out from the lianas, peeled in that massive slab of head poised among the leaves. After what seemed an eternity when he was utterly still, frozen in disbelief, and in awe, when for the first time he could recall nothing was moving in the world, Michael laughed softly, never shifting his mouth, a silent, mirthless laughter that ran through his whole body. Then he turned back the way he'd come.

As he made his way toward the village, he could no longer see her face. Nor could he find the picture of his toppled rig. Even the sound of the villagers had droned off to nothing. The road had fallen away. From the long night that only now ended—with the sun streaming bright green—but somehow had taken his lifetime to pass, all he could remember was the forest. And the grave warnings of his father who had died not of the bushmaster but of malaria. Who had entered the deep green from the blue of the Caribbean and, after some point, never returned.

Then he flashed to the old man who, after everything, would be glad to see him. Who was now the age his father would have been. Even from so far away, he could still make out that old dreamer in his Hilux beneath the dark, close trees. As though he were gazing out at him across a gap in time. They would ride together toward the coast. Alive, he would sprawl out where she had sprawled out, in the back, with someone else driving and, while the old man rattled on and on, watch the forest around them, deep and dense and beautiful, slowly disappear.

THE CANOEIST

When Kathy saw the animal, she stopped the car. Her boyfriend, Paul, was in the vehicle but he'd been looking down at his phone.

"What the hell was that?" she breathed, though it wasn't a question. She was already thinking she knew what she'd seen. It was large, crossing the road, crouched low to the tarmac but large.

"I'll be right back," she told Paul and jumped out and ran to the guardrail. Below her, just reaching the base of the high berm of the road, was the animal. Perhaps twenty feet away almost straight down. It lifted its broad face, bringing up its eyes. She'd slowed to a walk and gone quiet before approaching the rail, but somehow it had sensed her. For what felt like a full minute, into a second minute, she held its stare and at some point, she decided again what she'd decided before when eye-locked with an animal, that she wouldn't be the one to look away.

Finally, it shifted its gaze toward the trees and then, as though unsure, angled thick shoulders to stare at her once more. The fur on its neck was clean and white and came flush with the jawline. A hint of black, almost invisible, shone in the pelage just above the throat.

Lynx, thought Kathy, following the long, thin tendrils extending the ears. It's a lynx.

When the animal began nosing around in the frozen grass, she motioned to Paul, who was still sitting in the car. Then the two of them stood together, watching the lynx pause to gaze upward, nose around some more, and make its way out through the frozen marsh.

"*Achah*," whispered Paul, shouldering closer. "Blends right in."

He turned and walked back to the vehicle but Kathy stared at the lynx until after it was gone, watching it slip between the cattails, seeing it enter the sagebrush, catching finally just the swatch of its backside, the plush knob of the tail drifting through deepening snow and vanishing, first to slow fragments then a gray movement and at last to the slight swaying, an intensity, in dense, tall, frost-stiffened thickets that stretched away toward the woods.

"Gone," she whispered, surprising herself.

But there was wind on the road, and she could hear nothing. So it was the fact she'd said it at all that stayed, but nothing else.

•

The last time she'd spoken with her father was a week earlier when she was out on the airport road. He had been demanding as usual on the phone, telling her what to do. She'd taken it in, trying to stay out of trouble. Saying she would do it all, not to worry. And she had done it. His funeral had been beautiful, full of light. She'd spoken in the church along with her brothers, each of them coming forward, one at a time, and addressing the crowd. Kathy had come last because she was the oldest. His only daughter, as he had reminded her many times. She'd stood before them all with the sun streaming onto their faces and said he was not the type to leave. Too stubborn. That her father, somewhere, was still around. She could feel it.

His hands on the day before the funeral, when they'd gathered as a family before the visiting hours, were cold and waxen in the coffin. The coffin itself was monstrous, a huge box full of colored velvet for him to lie inside. Kathy had touched those hands a final time and stared. She'd stood beside Paul and waited, for movement, she supposed. For breath. For something to react to. But her father stayed silent and still. So she left him there, looking back over her shoulder from varying distances, just to be sure.

Over that weekend there had been so many people in his big house, which sat like the ancient hull of a ship above the woods. One at a time or in small clumps, they came shuffling quietly out of his life, down the carpeted halls, and shook Kathy's hand. Some gazed benignly from across his large, overheated rooms. Others stood off to one side and took her in at an angle. A few walked straight into her heartsong, telling her things about herself, about him, about what he'd said with pride when she wasn't around. There were even one or two who smiled carefully as if nothing much had happened or, after his decade of illness, as if it hardly came as a surprise. His funeral, their eyes seemed to say, was not unlike the long train of his days bridged together by years, passing through hospitals and remissions then out through sleep, with the engineers working just ahead of the engine, feeding it, keeping its noise if not its power, moving the great, dark labor of her father slowly across the landscape.

Afterward, when the guests had gone, Kathy changed and took the dog and, together with Paul, slipped out the basement door into deep snow. It was nearly dusk. People were napping. The churchwomen who had come to prepare and serve food as a gesture of friendship to her mother were still milling about the kitchen. From outside, she could hear them wishing everyone well, giving the house a last fillip of life before they sought their cars in the driveway and, once the exhaust had plumed up and wraithed into the wind, they steered slowly away toward town.

Kathy turned toward the woods and once she and Paul and the dog, Orion, broke into the trees, they found the snow cached high in places. Orion plowed a wavering path, using his tail as a rudder. He was a snow dog. From the time he was a puppy, Kathy had scooped him up and snuck him out to the woods when she came for long weekends. As it was a cautious, indoor family, there was the fierce worry that Orion, if encouraged, would wander off through the trees once Kathy was gone and lose his bearings, or stumble into the river and freeze, or be snatched by a fisher or coyote, or, if things were to fall out worse, be ambushed at night in the woods by something no one had a name for.

Since they could little afford such a fate with Kathy's father suffering in his room and seeming buoyed by the presence of that romping ball of fur, she had watched the dog carefully in the forest. She'd taught him secretly about ice. Its brittle, crackling skin over water. In his first season of snowmelt, she had stripped down and, clutching Orion to her chest, shown him the hastening chill of the river. They'd drifted, submerged to their jaws around a deep, silted bend, the dog silent, pressed up against her, his eyes large and black and glistening.

She would run out in front that first winter with Orion, her father inside dying of slowness, and tear through the spruce forest, turning to see only the moist, dark muzzle working the world behind her, afloat in a vast horizontal curtain of snow. While he was a puppy with lion paws, she would lift Orion over fallen trees after stealing out into the gloaming. There were still old-growth logs in the forest they could crawl into together, she first then the dog, so even the hush of the woods disappeared. Orion would curve his paws and fall asleep at her neck, every so often looking straight into her, wetting her face with his muzzle to ensure they were both alive.

"He loves me," her father had explained, with searching eyes from his bed. His head only would move in such moments, those eyes tracing a long, slow arc across the ceiling before latching onto her gaze. "Who feeds you?" he would ask Orion once Kathy had brushed off the snow in the basement and dried the puppy as best she could and cleaned his paws of bark and leaves and carried him squirming up the narrow stairs to that stale, doomed room of hope.

•

Now she watched as Orion pursued muted scents at speed through the drifts, his heavy body gathered up over his nose. The dog was almost a hundred pounds. After two years on and off in the woods with Kathy, he was reasonably experienced. With her mother turning a blind, generous, worried eye, they'd spent long hours during her visits traversing ravines, crossing frozen rivers, getting lost together in storms, working backward as a team, staking out dens of snowshoe hares, flushing white-tailed deer from winterberry bushes and bronzed swamp bracken, following owls that flowed like silent barrels through tunnels of air.

"You two been out here a few times before?" laughed Paul, teasing her. "Sure knows his route."

He glanced over and cut himself off. "I'm so sorry."

Every so often, Orion would turn on his heels and search for Kathy until, gauging her direction of travel, convinced they were moving together, however far apart, he would return to his nose. As they drifted toward the river she was listening for the wind and looking for her father's eyes so blue and light after years of chemotherapy they were windows thrown open, not for an hour or a night, but whole seasons.

"You miss him?"

"I don't know. I don't miss him right now."

She could feel Paul studying her face in the low, marbled light.

"No, I guess not," he went on. "He can't take that stuff back. But given the chance, you're thinking he might?"

"Yeah, probably."

Paul stopped, releasing her hand.

"It's the funeral, I know." His voice was tense. "But honestly, how do you get there?"

Kathy turned to face Paul who was hard to see in that moment. She heard her own voice small and quiet in the woods, as if it belonged to someone else. She was thinking, as she spoke, of her father's mouth, mobile and large, spitting harsh words across a square, plastic table.

"So he was bitter with his speeches," she whispered now. "Talking behind our backs. Downplaying what we were good at. Trying different stuff to put us down. You know, hating. Fuming—"

She felt herself tighten. Paul, with a few questions, made everything threaten to crash. She was back in the coffee shop across from her father's office where, in a striped work suit, he'd told her he was removing her from his life. She'd taken a job that meant traveling overseas. Stupidly, she'd thought he might like her news. It was a good job, in disaster relief. She was strong, after all, adept at handling other people's setbacks and her own many screwups. But the fact that it meant working in the Middle East, in South Asia, that it entailed risks for a woman who was unmarried, alone, made him lash out instantly. He'd looked at her incredulously, citing her naivete, the pale color of her skin, then calling her names.

"Can't you see they'll seek you out?" he'd sneered. "You're a target. Look at you. Now work with people in this country, why don't you. Or be there for your family. But don't go off and play misguided hero."

"Honestly, it's not heroism." She'd searched for something recognizable in his eyes, but they'd narrowed, and his mouth curled so far she could see both rows of teeth. "Just trying to help people—probably no more dangerous than the outdoor trips I've done for years."

But that was the wrong thing to say. His sneer hung before her like it was drying on a line. He had long questioned her decisions. He'd hated her solo hikes in alpine ranges in Central Asia with a Thuraya phone, her free diving off the coasts of Hawaii and Chile and Namibia, often alone, and her desert trips where she'd bouldered unaccompanied in remote canyons in Utah, Arizona, and elsewhere, carrying an emergency beacon and packing in her supplies.

"Well, I won't take that on," he'd said once he'd let his body fall back in his chair. "I've told you all along this is wrong—throwing yourself out there with no safety net. And for what? For *nothing*. Now sometime you have to quit. So that's it—this is it. I'm drawing the line. I've done it and done it and done it—no more. Period. Can't and won't. Know that going in."

As Kathy had done ever since, she'd stayed silent in those moments, watching his face crank through stages of fury, seeing it grow massive, contort, then abruptly collapse.

"Right, no surprise, you're like this, so generous. But I'm sorry—he turned off lights in you that don't go back on."

Suddenly hearing Paul's voice, as if he'd walked up flush with her eyes, making her blink, she struggled against a new backfall into the reeling period that began when her father, six months after his declaration in the coffee shop, was diagnosed with cancer.

"Look, I'm sure he did," she said now. "I'm sure I'm not the same because of him. I'm not arguing with any of that. But here's the thing. In the last two years he saw me again, my strength, my athleticism, my loyalty."

"Achah, come on. You climbed out and cleaned his roof gutters. And sprinted with his dog. And got things done around his house other people wouldn't or couldn't."

"The thing is—" And she scanned the drifts between the trees, searching for Orion. "When he looked at you, all the bad stuff—he could take that away."

For a moment Paul moved toward her. He was thick in this too. Staggering a little, unsure of his steps. Then he choked back a sob.

"No," she went on, the word sounding all-at-once and loud. "He could look at you and *see* you. I never said anything to him. But in those last two years he *looked* at me—he saw me."

Paul wavered in the dusk, a filament flickering against the polished hush of the woods. He seemed to be waiting for his voice so it would not betray him.

"Right," he croaked. "Sure. And for your sake, believe me, I hope that's true."

•

Kathy had met Paul, who was Pakistani, during her second year away, on an aid project in the earthquake recovery zone just east of the Indus River and south of Besham. Paul's Pashtun family was from Gulberg, a wealthy district of Lahore, and he'd been educated in England though his parents had never left Pakistan. They owned a trout farm on a milky blue tributary of the Swat River, along with a cement factory that imported stone and marble from Tora Bora in Afghanistan and squatted just outside the busy, exhaust-ridden *chowk* in Mardan.

Paul, Kathy thought from the beginning, was hard to place in terms of ethnicity, motive, and origin. He'd struck her initially as deeply ambitious and worldly in ways that made her skeptical. Yet when he invited her north and they'd jeeped up the long dirt road beside the Swat River from Mingora to Kalam, she met his generous, enlivening mother who was constantly in motion and who ran a girls' school during the summers in a small shack on the slopes above the river.

Paul's father, alongside his other ventures, owned a three-room inn, catering mainly to domestic tourists from Sindh Province far to the south who trickled in, tired and dusty, smelling of goat and the black smoke of Karachi. For three summers, Kathy and Paul hiked and climbed through fir and blue spruce forests around Desan Mountain and Falak Sair on the southern spur of the Hindu Raj Range. While Paul was strong and persevering in alpine conditions, he admitted from the outset, with a mouth perfectly straight and kind, that he'd rather be in London, Paris, or New York.

So after five years of traveling back and forth, Kathy returned with him to the United States and continued work for the aid agency from a desk job in Boston. The disaster relief projects still took her away, sometimes for several months, but Paul began a graduate program in international relations and, after three semesters, flew back to north Pakistan for stints of field work. Alone, or with Paul when they were both stateside, Kathy would drive up to New Hampshire to see her parents. As things played out, her father hadn't gone so far as to boycott her presence. For the five years she spent overseas and on the road, he'd received her visits in variable moods, mostly subdued, with intermittent fits of invective. He'd shaken his head and muttered expletives, characterized her as irresponsible and untrustworthy, and painted her as a maverick. But Kathy weathered it, refusing to give him up despite Paul's protestations. Once in a while, her father would plunge through his fear and the anger and smile in his old way, compliment her on her sports in the backyard, or hug her all of a sudden as if his frail frame would break.

Even now, all those trips home stood in the shadow of her first Christmas with Paul after eight months of their dating in Islamabad and Kalam. She'd flown back with him for the winter holidays and things had fallen out badly. Her father had taken Kathy aside and explained her misunderstanding of cultural perceptions; her failure to see Paul's interest in US citizenship; the hardship she brought on them all by aligning herself with someone outside her upbringing; the disgrace she embodied by living with him unmarried overseas where, he claimed, she could get away with it because there was less scrutiny and lower standards. Finally, the danger she embraced, the risks she took not only through her job but through her month-long trips into mountains, rainforests, and deserts, made it clear she was lost, both deeply confused and irresponsible. "That man you are with," he had admitted, "cannot be blamed for this last part."

Paul was outraged when he heard, vowing never to return, claiming no one should be subjected to such distortions or to this kind of repeated, manipulative abuse.

"You're an aid worker," he'd yelled in the car afterward, hearing Kathy's softened version of her father's speeches, then pounding the steering wheel. "You should be recognized, not attacked. For God's sake, you try to *help* people. And you take risks, more than I'd like, but you take risks because you're courageous."

He had paused, struggling to get ahold of himself, pivoting his lanky body to face her in the cramped vehicle.

"Look, I'm sorry, but that man is deeply screwed up. What he's doing would not be tolerated somewhere else. You can't just take it all like you're immortal. Nobody, Kathy, not even you, can take everything, again and again, without getting damaged."

But Kathy had just shrugged and taken it anyway. For years, the visits were like boxing matches in which she would stand before her father with her gloves down. She specialized, she'd joke to Paul, in taking beatings. "Why do you let him say that stuff?" a few curious members of the family would ask. Some of them clearly assumed it was all true, while Paul, swearing he could take it no longer, that if she didn't speak up, then by God he'd do it for her, turned colors of rage and lifted his hands above his head.

Though he wasn't practicing, Paul was Muslim, and many of his mannerisms came from his mother who was not permitted, as a woman, into the mosque in Kalam but who prayed fervently at home, in the courtyard beneath freighted walnut trees, in her busy kitchen, or in an alcove where Kathy could watch from the layered rugs of the sitting room. Paul, when he was upset, would roll his eyes toward the sky just like his mother, almost comically except that it was not comical, and beseech mercy and patience. Or he would lower his forehead as she did in prayer, with devotion and gravity. "*Al-Hamdu lillah*," he would mutter, then stare out the window of the car distractedly until Kathy grabbed the wheel and reminded him he was driving.

"Don't call him on it," she would whisper in these moments.

"He's very sick. I watch while he's making those speeches, his mouth curled up and leering, and I wait for it all to be a dream. For him to wake up first. I keep thinking he'll shake himself, then reach over and touch my arm. But he never does."

"Look, don't speak. Honestly, I can't hear this anymore. He's desperate and bitter. You're crazy. We're both crazy. I drive you up there and every time I have to say it right here. On this same road."

Paul, in his protectiveness and disbelief, his exasperation, would point at something, some kind of landmark, a stand of balsam or a dying white pine or a roadside flange of flattened cattails and say, "This swamp, yes, *exactly* this swamp. I'm always *right* here in the swamps, five minutes out on *this road* after we leave those outrageous, defaming speeches, and I'm already telling you I will never in my life drive to that horrible place again."

•

Now Paul turned and began trudging back, stepping into his own prints. Kathy watched first him then the dog, who were one hundred eighty degrees apart. Snow had begun to fall and an old blue light rose from the ground to sift through the trees. She could no longer feel her father up in the house as she had in the past from the woods. The enormous, rickety structure contained other sleepers, or people who were just now awakening, or small, hesitant conversations that, she imagined, were not yet real to anyone. Later, they would sit around a wooden table and have beers or milk. Light would pour onto their faces while one after the other they spoke. So, collectively, they could try to understand things. But for now, the difference between those dark rooms and the surrounding world must be minimal. Though she was too deep in the woods to see the house, she thought of it as sealed off, a still place, which couldn't possibly play host to light and bore no switches at all.

Orion, far out in front, was headed for the deer bridge. Trudging behind him, she glimpsed it finally, shaping and releasing the air. Though she couldn't see them, beyond the old wooden bridge the river dove into the falls. Then boiled downstream and pooled in dark water. In late spring, after the last snowmelt carrying mud and slurry, the river ran through broad and clear. But now the eddies were frozen. In midwinters like these, you could walk out on cold mornings after a night snow had fallen, windless and straight, and find deep, crystalline tracks of deer on the bridge, mostly does and fawns moving without haste, or the spray-encased, hustling spoor of a fox. Kathy had wondered while her father was alive if the derelict bridge, with its freight of new snow, would finally collapse beneath her through the glassy meringue of the river so she would come back to him dripping, hued pale like he was.

Now when she turned short of the bridge, having called back the dog, and made her way up to the house that gleamed with electricity on a hill overlooking the woods, she saw it as full of light. But when she stepped in, everything was dim and hushed. The kitchen was clean, tidy, with piles of things silent on the counters, and when she'd climbed the dark, narrow stairs she found Paul lying in the stillness of their bedroom.

"You're back," he whispered.

"Yes, I've toweled off Orion."

"The smell in here—those flowers. You can't get away from it."

"I know."

When Kathy turned on the lamp by the bed she saw Paul had been crying.

“Terrible, isn’t it?” he choked out, too loudly, so she stepped back as her eyes adjusted, then came forward again and lay tightly beside him on the bed.

“I keep thinking about the baseball,” he went on.

Kathy smiled because Paul, as a cricketer, had loved the baseball. Her father was a graceful left-handed pitcher throughout his life, well into his illness, and Kathy, because of her speed, was always his single outfielder in the games in the yard. Up through his last game, she would snare balls on a dead run or after long dives deep in his outfield, and as she rose from the grass her father would shake his head and call out, “Routine fly ball,” to bring guffaws from their guests. Always, he had been a fantastic joker, a mimic of sorts, who could stand on the mound and throw unhittable slowballs to all of them, making brilliant, grotesque faces at the batters that brought them to the ground with laughter.

Despite everything, Paul had returned to the house again and again during their years in Boston before her father’s death, and the one thing that seemed to soften his ire were the ballgames. Paul was tall and athletic, and in England and Islamabad he had been an avid cricketer and played in university leagues. Her father, she could tell, admired this about him. They were two natural men on the field, chatting with one another, looking knowingly at the opposition, adjusting their positions with a glance at each other. Ballgames, which were constant and loved by her father, formed a strange oasis from which Paul would come away admiring the heavy American bats, pounding his fist into American mitts, and throughout the years when her father could still stand waveringly and pitch, Paul would grin at the unhittable balls and colorful rhetoric that came from the mound. After those at-bats, Paul would sit on the grass staring at her father, first in disbelief, then with a merry kind of laughter very much his own that came out in bursts and ended in a slow-fading smile.

"Why couldn't he just do *that*? I mean, that was—unbelievable. He was brilliant."

"I know," whispered Kathy. "I wish."

"Yeah, but do you think *he* wished?"

"You've asked me that."

"Right, because I don't get it. I'm trying to understand."

"You're amazing," she said. "If anyone could get it, trust me, you would."

Paul paused for a second in the darkness of the room and Kathy could feel the snow falling outside invisibly and the dog downstairs heavy and asleep by the door to the stairs, sunk in the smells of the woods, and the people of the house gathering in its corners to touch each other or speak of the long winter, and her father, mute and still at the funeral home, not sleeping inside of time, waiting for the thaw so they could break the earth and bury him.

"What I do know is—I wish he were alive right now," Paul went on, tearing up again. "Over in that horrible, horrible room."

•

That night, after the stories and beer, Kathy dreamed of him. Her father was in a canoe and slowly losing steam. She was searching for him with Orion. Somehow, they were in the woods while her father was stranded on a vast, smooth plane of water.

"We have to find the lake," she was shouting to Orion, who seemed frenzied, beyond himself. "Follow the river. There isn't much time." And as she ran through the snow and broke out of the trees, she could see even at a distance her father was freezing cold. He was paddling still, away from heavy falls, trying to reach an eddy. But as had been the case for years, there was so little flesh on his bones. His thigh, exposed to the wind and jutting against her vision above the rim of the canoe, was angular, scarcely more than the bone-knife of the femur.

For a moment Orion hesitated when they reached the shore. There was ice and she'd taught him to be wary. But when she never broke stride, when she leapt from the woods and crashed out onto the ice, the dog was beside her in a moment and the two of them were racing across, their feet and paws here or there breaking through. Her father had seemed closer when she'd first hit the ice but now that gap was growing. Nonetheless, she could still see his body if not his face, the taut wires of his frame, his fast grip on the paddle, the desire he carried in place of strength.

"I've got you, Dad," she was yelling. "Just hang on."

"I'm not going to be able to hang on," he was saying hoarsely in a voice scarcely above a whisper but that reached her somehow, carried by the wind, and spurred them, Orion and her. "So dammit, don't risk yourself."

But as she'd done for so long, Kathy was ignoring his advice, shooting for the canoe, gunning for him with everything she had. Her lungs were straining in the cold air.

"For once in your life, goddammit, stop trying to be the heroine. Stop proving yourself out here."

Now she hit the floe edge where the frigid current was rushing toward the falls and, again, without breaking stride, stretched her body into a long, flat dive.

For an instant Kathy thought about the dog while she was still underwater. But when she lifted toward the surface to breathe and submerged again, she decided she couldn't do everything at once and pulled with her arms for the drifting canoe.

"Keep pulling," she sputtered to both her father and herself, though her mind had gone empty with cold and she could see next to nothing but roaring colors shot through with spray.

"Just hang on." But she was speaking now mostly underwater, opening her eyes onto green cold, then rising like a dolphin out into the air and calling against the wind so, if anything, her voice trailed backward into the woods.

"You're doing this for yourself, not for me," he was saying, his eyes grayed out by sky. "Don't you get it? I *can't* hang on."

Once she got to the canoe just before it swept over the falls, towed it somehow from the main throat of the current and hauled it across the eddies toward the ice, she could feel nothing in her body, nearly frozen. Still, before she lifted herself out of the water, she swam back behind it and began to push, to secure the bow on the floe edge so that he didn't drift off, so, having been close in their lives once before, they didn't lose each other all over again.

"See," she gasped, when his canoe was secure, when she was still immersed to the neck, tilting her jaw to breathe. "You didn't believe."

But after Kathy had hoisted her shoulders, dragged her hips up onto the ice, managing to roll herself out of the lake like a seal, and had crawled at last to the canoe and begun towing it slowly, painfully toward the shore, she looked back behind her and saw it was empty. Perhaps always had been empty.

•

"What is it?" Paul grunted. "What the hell is wrong with you?"

Kathy was clambering over his body toward the door, falling from the bed and crashing against the lamp in the darkness on the way to the floor. In a split second, she was up.

"Where's Orion?" she hissed.

"The dog? He's asleep. Come on, calm down."

"No, no, where's Orion *right* now?"

"The dog's asleep, Kathy. We were all asleep a minute ago."

Then she felt Orion against her thighs, roughing her, bringing his lion paws up nearly to her chest.

"Oh god, I was sure I'd left him out there. I thought he'd drowned."

"Well apparently, he's here. It was a dream. So why don't you both come back over. Slowly this time."

Kathy found the lamp on the floor and righted it and padded around the room and climbed back into the high bed. In another moment, Orion was walking on top of them and circling sleepily before returning to his deep, warm hollow near their knees.

"I'm so sorry."

"It's okay, honestly. Always so calm. Never any emotion. Unless you're mad." Paul laughed softly in the dark until they both laughed. "Then you're horrible," he whispered, wringing his hands above them. "You get that from him."

"Yes, very bad."

"And when you dream. Achah, I've never met anyone who has your dreams. Usually at three a.m."

"Well, I hope not."

Kathy moved closer to Paul and buried her feet beneath Orion, to warm them from a cold that now, she imagined, was everyone's cold, that swept up the river to the room where heaters had spewed while her father lay trembling and surveying it all, even his mind, with a sour vigilance he alone could muster. Now, tonight, that same cold sifted its way down the hall beneath the door into her bones and she could feel him through the woodwork, the dark silence that wrapped his eyes, the long years he'd followed into suffering and that made him stare at her finally, too weak or too tired for all his old words, seeing her at last, or so she wanted so badly to believe—that having started to haul him to safety, then turning to find nobody in his canoe, she'd climbed in herself and taken up his paddle and begun slowly to row across the ice.

•

They stayed for another two days until everyone was gone, then said goodbye to her mother who hadn't slept in a week and was beginning to doze on her feet among the rows of flowers as she walked in the hallway, peering from one bouquet to another, studying the names, rereading small messages, pausing now and again to bring her face up close to the winterberries or to softly press the pussy willows. As Kathy and Paul made their way out, she was lurching toward a chair beside a vase of ashen chrysanthemums whose stems, from across the room, seemed to come from her closing eyes. Once Kathy had shut the door behind them, Orion reared up on his hind legs inside and pounded his forepaws and chest, then finally his head, against its glass pane.

"That dog," said Paul, glancing back.

"Oh I know—I hear. I explained everything to him. But now I can't look."

Kathy, who was at the wheel so Paul could work, drove out

toward the highway but didn't make it that far. She stopped the car five minutes from the house. And as Paul walked back to the vehicle, having stood alongside her to watch the lynx trail off into the brush, he called over his shoulder that they should get home. It was late. There was a long drive ahead.

"I have work to do tomorrow," he said. "So do you. Remember?"

But after years of dating the same man, Kathy listened instinctively to Paul's voice rather than to his words because even now, as she wavered, that voice remained gentle and even. And when she saw the lynx disappear in the direction of the woods, she meant to heed his good advice and turn back to the car and resume driving toward their lives, to thank Paul far out on the highway, beyond his dread swamps and landmarks, for being there so long. Yet she stood against the wind another whole moment once she'd said, "Gone," allowing it to echo soundlessly. Then, without turning, she climbed over the rail and slid down the iced berm.

"Kathy," she heard Paul yelling out across the frozen swamp. "What in God's name are you doing?"

But she believed he understood what she was doing. No doubt better than she did. He was amazing in that way.

"Your father's nowhere out there, al-Hamdu lillah. You've seriously got to let him go. Now please, please come back to the car."

On more than one occasion, Paul's mother had gravely explained that she'd given him an English name because otherwise he would never leave her, and she'd grown certain now he would never leave Kathy because he'd climbed mountains with her, which no one had convinced him to do before. In any case, since Kathy was sure he'd be there, asleep in the passenger seat with headphones slipping off his ears; knees crammed up on the dash; and long legs, mantis-like, bent over the gear shift, the keys still dangling from the ignition, she hastened her step in the sinking light and began to pursue the lynx, as if those deep prints led back to the house that at dusk would glow already like a wild heart from within.

"You know like I do he's nowhere out there. Now come on. Achah, there's no more you can do. It's over. You survived it all."

Kathy could hear Paul hollering from the high berm of the road over one of his swamps until she'd tracked the lynx deep into the woods, after it had grown fully dark and she'd lost the spoor and was doubling back, then working in long circles down the grade toward the river. Who knew where she was going? She shivered. If anybody could save him, she believed her father had known, she would be the one.

And as she made her way farther through the snow, she imagined carrying him all bundled across the deer bridge, hoisting her father's frail, skeletal frame onto her shoulders. She would show him, even now, the places where whitetails bedded down in shallower drifts, away from the wells of trees but inside the breadth of their sloping branches. They were like caves, these places high in the pine woods, and she would skirt curved imprints left by the deer's warm, folded bodies. Then, having reached exhaustion, she would lift him through lonesome miles of moose country, their minds aflame together in the wind, and rather than ask the question Paul had posed, would he take it all back, descend into muskeg in the wake of that night of portage to bear him where there was no bridge and she was his only canoe, across a colder, darker, deeper river just beyond her strength.

THREE PARTS OF HUNGER

The lion we called the "old man" was rail thin with ribs bulging like so many horns of animals he had devoured in a deep past that no longer belonged to him. He stretched his mangled neck forward and raised his lower jaw, dipping his heavy cranium briefly toward the ground, so he would send his call out low across the land. Though his strong voice caromed, the scrub brush, the fossil river, the challenge of hills, even the loose sand itself all marred the sound as it wavered across the dune slopes. And the dry desert air made a poor vessel for that bellow. So during our first week at Bape when I would lie alone in the tent, listening, betting he was off patrolling the still distances, I'd be wrong. Instead, before I could move, the lion would be twelve feet out and his slow-swaying yellow eye would oval vertically too high above the dark earth for me to call, "Brown hyena, you," whose eyes at night are nearly green or, "Black-backed jackal with your silver flare," whose glance is ripped with motion.

For most of that first week, on nights when the old man was nearby, Molly slept in the truck parked beside a haggard puzzle bush. I'd feel her stiffen beside me as his slow bark of groans began to track across the veld. She would wait for that call to come twice. The third time, she would rise, shimmy over my hips, and unzip the screen. Without a word, she would step briskly into the flip-flops awaiting her feet and pad over to the truck. I'd hear the creak of the passenger door. Then I would picture her crawling into the back cab, squeezing her narrow body between jerricans, spreading out as best she could. She must have curled her long, freckled legs around those cans brimful of diesel and listened all night to the muted hills because in the mornings she would say, her voice cranked low and short of water, thinning already toward something close to desperate, "You know, he was here with us all night."

•

From the day she laid eyes on his wounds and gasped, Molly kept her gaze fixed somewhere in the distance unless the old man was around. We would sit up on the hood of the truck, parceling out lentils or beans, and she would stare into the trough between the hills. The few times our spoons would meet just above the can, she would lift hers abruptly away. The skies had begun changing even back then. Lofty cumulus clouds came sailing into view by two in the afternoon and by six we would hear thunder in the distance to the north. What's more, wispy shreds of moisture trailed low in the skies, what they called mare's tails in America, forming with greater frequency, and earlier.

Rain would dampen the sand and initially make passage north far easier. But we understood, both of us, that once we got onto the northern plateau, it would be a different story. The mud could get heavy if the rains persisted. And if the rains did come in earnest, they would transform the stiff mineral pans of the central Kalahari into broad soft lakes of standing water that could swallow a truck or, once they had stretched beyond their margins, become nearly impassable. I'll admit, as time crept on at Bape and as Molly grew thinner and began to change, this possibility weighed upon me. I'd frequently glance up to watch the skies, and at night even allow myself the warming delusion that we had already left and I had won a great battle of wills.

In the mornings during that first week, we would drive out looking for the old man and the young male that had tried to kill him on the night we had arrived. On our first night at Bape in the hours before dawn we had heard the usual low moans to mark territory or call females. Then silence we couldn't interpret and a more guttural set of noises. They began as brief, jagged snarls and changed abruptly to what sounded not like lions at all but the shaking of canteens partially filled with sand. Twice, roars we never heard again tore the night. Later, during long stillness, I whispered to Molly that perhaps hyenas were challenging for a kill. But even after it turned cool and we were deep in our bags, rolling in and out of sleep, we never once heard the low gruff challenge of hyenas. Just the lonely quavering story of the jackal aloft in the dark air.

The next morning, we had driven out in the direction of the noise and found the lions in a high clearing commanding a strip of veld curling off toward a broad fossil riverbed. It was gruesome. The old man was nearly dead. It had been a war, perhaps with his son. In any case with a known lion because they lay afterward in the same field. The young one with a brief tawny mane reposed among the lionesses beneath sparse gray ruins of camel thorn, while the old man lay sprawled at some distance, alone in the merciless sun. A wound cut into his right eye until it had partially closed, then ripped out along the brim of his skull above the ear. A brilliant flash of blood had congealed there and, where it was thickest, lay coating his dark mane. The eye itself when it came open was shot through with the color of jujube, of the bright red of the ziziphus tree which in places around us was beginning to fruit. At the end, the younger lion had held the old man's head in his jaws, pinning him no doubt after coming along his neck from behind. A deeper wound poured onto the ground from the old man's thick left foreleg that, as though broken, lay angled unnaturally against the grain of his flanks.

Then, on the second day, we had watched him heave up unsteadily onto his haunches and prove he was not yet dead. That night he had hobbled close to our camp and slept on the dry hummock behind the truck. By the fourth afternoon, the young male also had left the clearing, and through much of the night he called from the hills around us, tracing his slow perimeter and scent marking in the dark.

"That young one's thinking our old man's too weak to give him trouble," whispered Molly in the tent while the young male was roaming. "What with all those females lying around."

An hour or so later, as though she'd gone right on talking, she rose up on her elbows and woke me. When I opened my eyes, Molly was zoomed in. The moon slicked her face.

"I'm sick with it, Jake."

•

Several evenings later, still lingering at Bape, when we drove back to our camp, the skies had thickened noticeably. Dusk came at once. Thunder boomed across the veld to the north. While I pulled long sickles of acacia thorns out of our tires and began silent preparations for a morning departure, Molly made none.

Once the wind was up and sifting through the tent screen, she began softly to predict things. Maybe, she whispered, the lionesses would take an oryx while we slept. There had been many at Bape in those days before the rains. To the north, in the great northern valleys of the Central Kalahari Game Reserve, the springbok and blue wildebeest herds would be gathering drowsily in the evenings to sleep on broad damp pans and riverbeds. But here in the dry south, in this remote section of scrub, Bape belonged to the oryx, with their long spearing horns and masked faces. Here was thick bush and dune veld, the sand alternating from bleached white to a deep crayoned red, combed in the hills with brown and mineral black. So the oryx could hide.

Perhaps, as Molly told it, the big lioness would be famished after her long sessions of mating with the young male that had lasted, on and off, for many hours and parts of two days. Possibly, when the moon blinked, that lioness would creep onto the veld and pull an oryx from this world. Then the old man would edge forward from the slip of hills where we had made camp and spread his one strong eye upon her until she backpedaled and withdrew. He'd bend slowly and draw in the flesh of that kill with his jaws working. Afterward he would allow it to spread inside him while he settled back into the thick bushman grass. As he rested, that same flesh would fall along the spaces in his skeleton and at last approach his ribs.

I said nothing to Molly, but the truth was when we had last glimpsed the old man, his belly hung like an empty bag and his behind was a narrowing blade. Anyone could see that his steps, with the mangled leg a strange sorrow in his gait, came slow and specific and shattered.

During the night, once Molly was talked out, the lion must have stayed close because on waking we found his strange broken track through camp. He had passed by the truck so tightly, it appeared, as to brush it with his flanks. Yet unlike previous nights, either his passage had been soundless or we had been deeply asleep, and Molly had remained in the tent.

"I won't leave. Not until he's dead or we've seen that leg through," she announced quietly at dawn, bending over his spoor and fingering the pug marks.

She was brushing her teeth without water. Molly, in the wilderness, has always been a dark, hopeful saver of water. "Drink, Molly," I'd say on such mornings. "We've brought plenty." Then, after her raw silences, "You can even shower lightly from the drum if you'd like. Besides, now the rains are close." Following these speeches, I'd hoist the water drum theatrically and allow a trickle to splat on my brow then, before it could intensify, tilt my head forward to let it roll across my eyes.

But now I just stared at Molly's slim back hunched over the broken spoor of the old man. Her Irish shoulders, twice peeled, were a deeply mottled brown. She looked narrow as a thorn.

"Can't stay forever," I told her. "Yeah, we've still got the water," and she looked up to gaze at me blankly. "But our food's nearly gone."

Up until then, for most of the long month we had already spent in the Kalahari, Molly had been the one constantly ushering us on, pushing me hard to cover ground, to cross the scrub desert before our supplies drew down to nothing, to "get north" and be out the other side. "There's nothing here," she would say, her voice high and worried. "It's empty." And she had come back to the dust and the monotony, to her stated desire to have done with the dry lands.

Now Molly looked down at the lion tracks. "You know I won't leave," she said softly.

•

The old man walked into camp like a ghost out of that dawn. Stepping from the blackthorn and moving in the early heat before he was real. He was a shadow, then a moment of his one strong eye, then the shrugging wag of his head that hung beneath his shoulders and followed them, unwillingly it seemed, wherever they went.

Now they came toward us. As though it were the hidden chest steering. My own eyes were still wet with water I'd poured across them to clear the night. Molly had swallowed rather than spat and was returning her toothbrush to the small folder of personal gear she kept like a tiny treasury in her corner at the back of the truck bed. I must have caught her with my stillness because she turned to find the lion directly before her.

He veered as she turned and arced around the far side of the truck until I lost sight of him. Molly, I could see, was herself blocked by the rear door that had swung out. She wheeled toward me. *Where is he now?* She stood, yelling in silence, shrinking back toward the truck, her round face pulled taut, the long, loose black hair pushed rapidly aside, eyes fierce but comically apart.

In the meantime, the old man must have paused behind the vehicle. Then there he was, materializing out from his jaw and limp forepaw. In another moment he was in front of the truck grill, tilted to one side, weighting his strong right leg. The black mane that is the signature of the male Kalahari lion hung deeply along his neck and onto the crest of his spine and spilled down well below his shoulders, merging finally with the tawny, nearly colorless shag that lay beneath it. He hadn't eaten. He was the lion-headed sheath for a blade.

Molly must have watched me take him in because at first, she didn't move. Then after a moment, she began to step lightly toward me across the dust. The one good yellow eye in that dawn went on staring and came nearly brown in the pale light. The massive head shifted slowly toward us as dark candle thorn trees rose out of his back. After another step, the stiff white prongs of acacia shrubs glowed behind the bell tuft of his tail.

Lions, my father used to say, find in human beings an abiding mystery. They know we can kill them, but they don't know how. They view us, normally, from behind long stares. This lion, moreover, looked scarcely able to bear his own weight.

Now Molly edged in tightly beside me. When the old man failed to react to her appearance, she crouched low. He shifted his gaze briefly to her face before turning and dragging his narrow back up the dry hummock into the trees. She remained there motionless for a long time, well after his gray silhouette had merged with the blackthorn, and I realized the whole time I had faced him I was struggling to commit him to memory.

•

"I'd say we've water enough for a week and could still get out," Molly whispered, as we drove from camp toward the clearing split-wired with ghosts where we had first found the old man.

"That's if nothing goes wrong from here," I told her. "Three days north from Bape. Then another seven hours, depending on rain, to make petrol and your chocolate in Rakops. That's if they've stocked diesel. And if the rains on the plateau don't shut us down."

"I've no more need of chocolate," she smiled wanly. "And the rains will be water."

We had scarcely left camp and turned down the dirt track to the south when we found the old man splayed in a bank of sharp-spiked yellow blooms beneath a candle pod tree. These trees of the Kalahari spread far before they arch down to graze the sand. My mother called them "houses of the lion" because, as a young woman on safari with her uncles, she would find whole prides resting, even turned on their backs with legs slung in the air, inside the deep shaded recesses. Now the long greenish pods formed a candelabra above the old man. His head, carrying its bright eye, rose out of the blooms to float strange and momentous among so many small things. Then, almost immediately, it wobbled, lolled sideways, and crashed hard into the sand.

"Hyenas will take him," I told Molly as we drove back. "No need to wait around."

Growing up in South Africa, in the northwest of the country that forms the southern margin of the desert, I was taught hyenas take everything eventually. That the San down through the millennia, when their elders were too weak to keep up, would build thatched shelters and surround them with sharp limbs of blackthorn against all comers—to parry killers and scavengers in general, but especially hyenas.

"So they could die in peace," I had explained to Molly years before, when I was wooing her outside of Albany, New York, seeking to use my birth in Africa as a way to lure her, to promise her things I've never, honestly, felt I contain.

"They would give these elderly people supplies, of course. They would leave behind what water and food they could spare," I had gone on.

Yet this, we were warned, was only a gesture. After a few days or a week, well before the water stored in ostrich eggshells had run out, the hyenas would chase a lone leopard away in the hours before dawn and stalk those old San asleep in their thorns. They'd come right through the brush barrier, first one, then in numbers. By sunrise, it was said, they'd have chewed their old bones to chalk.

•

As on previous evenings, I parked the truck behind our gnarled puzzle bush, half-eaten by fire of the dry months. The thunder had grown louder and more insistent each night, a sharp wrist moving from lid to lid, cracking open tight jars of sky. That night it grew closer until, in under an hour, its long train of labor halted at our tent sleeve and enveloped us. Lightning began to strike, close enough for us to feel it in our arms and see the hairs on them unsettle and rise. Each time a bolt lit us up, the yellow vault of the tent flashed brightly, spreading above us a round of electric light with long, jagged trees tilted on it.

Despite all this, it did not rain. It was a grayer sunrise, and the thickness of night lingered more strongly, and longer, but there was nothing else to distinguish that dawn from any other. When I emerged, the old man was lying by the rear wheel of the truck, his gaze locked on my movement. He must have approached during the thunder and was somehow larger for his state of emaciation, as though his chassis were only now visible without the bulked flesh to hide its length.

I retraced the few steps I'd taken, then changed my mind, coming around to stand between him and the tent.

"Molly," I said softly. "Your lion is here."

There was no fear. We knew each other already in this way, without truck doors or tent walls to separate us. I was aware, of course, that he was urgently hungry. While there was nothing to suggest aggression, all of it could alter in an instant. I waited for a long time, for separate seconds, for the old man to move or decide on something. But lions on the ground, if you don't advance or change, will normally outwait you.

I heard Molly come out from the tent and motioned stillness to her. She ignored me, walking steadily past, leaning far forward, as though she had snuck money from a wallet and was making for a tight door.

The old man left me with his eyes and shifted them to her legs. His whole head moved to make this change. His forepaws were stretched flat in front of his chest and he was parallel to the truck, looking sideways at her across a shoulder that had shriveled to a jut of bone.

"Molly, this lion's here because he's desperate." I hissed each word separately. "You're misreading him."

She kept on as though I had been silent. I wavered, wary of moving in and pulling her back for fear of startling the old man and confusing things, of confirming the moment as a challenge. Molly crouched down fifteen feet from the lion. He looked at her intently, changing nothing in his gaze, but following her body as it compressed. When she began to speak, his curved ears shifted abruptly in a tight arc, one more fully than the other.

"Don't be afraid, old man," she said. "I'm like you are."

"Molly," I stood hissing.

He left her with his gaze and brought it toward my voice.

"We're all right," she went on, and the old man came back to her face with his one tall, perfect eye. "Nothing's changed."

Then she began to cry. I could tell she was crying when she came to "changed" because the word came out muffled and twanging. She looked miniature before him, a little girl, her soft, browned neck bent forward beneath strands of black, wild-strewn hair.

"Don't sit down," I whispered more gently. "At least keep your knees up toward him."

The lion had shifted. Somewhere in the instant I had left him with my eyes at the sound of Molly's emotion, he had edged his paws in closer to his face and half risen. He hunched his shoulders in now and lifted himself gingerly, the dark black mane washing over him from this new angle and hiding the upper ridge of his back. He hung there on rickety haunches, tall and wasted.

"Now ease back real slowly," I whispered. "Show him your height. Just raise up a little at a time."

Molly shrank herself down.

"You've said it to him, baby. Now you've got to come back to *me*."

The old man didn't move. By this point, he stared only at her, his body dead square to hers, weighting his forepaws, even when I spoke.

"Don't hunt me, lion," Molly whispered.

•

The truth is the old man must have been weaker and more wretched than we thought. Rather than the single motion I've often seen with lions who, startled or half asleep, rise to reposition themselves in the shifting pattern of shade beneath a solitary mopane tree, this lion had many parts that looked as if they would creak and split apart as he stood. Nonetheless, when he was up, the curve of his great head flowed above the hood line of our truck.

He stepped toward Molly, shifting away from the damaged leg that seemed to have worsened over these nights. The blood was gone. But while his paw met the sand squarely, he flashed his hip away from the pain at each hesitant step, weighting himself to the right like a listing galley.

"No," I barked, and his head swung out toward me, the jaw dipping slightly. He was breathing to cool himself. After a brief pause, he began moving in on her again.

"Molly, please bring your knees up *now* and slowly stand."

She stayed where she was. Once the lion had halved the distance between them, she sat down altogether.

He stood for a moment, smelling her. He leaned his muzzle toward her, stretching it far out over his good right leg. He breathed her in deeply, craning his long neck so it came in line with his back. His head alone moved forward until it looked to be suspended nearly above her.

"Please don't, Jacob. Don't come, don't come."

And in that instant, as I was moving in to end it, it sounded to me as if she were singing.

•

I halted when she asked, poised to spring. I don't know why I heeded her. I know I wished for my father's hunting rifle as I stood before the tent through long moments of that dawn that stretched years of my sawyer's life in America until they snapped to this far place. I'd shoot into the air and send the lion ambling off. Then hunt game and bring him back to strength. If I were of an older race of men, I'd follow the spoor of an oryx through silky bushman grass and lunge into its night lair. Then spin a bright awl of terminalia onto corkwood to make fire. Rather than ignite just the gut-song of the truck each afternoon.

But much in those moments was given to my mind by my mother's volumes on the wit of Zambian giraffe hunters. And her library of bush tales stored to this day in a shipping container in Dedham, Massachusetts. And by the truth that, since I moved to America when my father died in a mine near Jwanang, I've missed Africa so horribly it remains a stolen scalding interior, giving a hole when I touch it and making me crash against Molly at night.

While I paused, the old man raised his injured leg and left it in the air. He had changed again in the face, wrinkling it to a kind of sneer, and it was higher, poised suddenly above his shoulders. The mouth came unset, jaw unslung, and lower teeth were white and visible. As he cut into the remaining distance that separated him from Molly, his limp hitched and smoothed out, all but disappearing.

"Don't come don't come," Molly was humming, perhaps to us both.

By then I'd edged forward, preparing as a last resort to jump him. To rely on his weakness which seemed, despite his size, bottomless and destroying.

"Please—now you mustn't move at all," I whispered.

The old man stood directly before her and sniffed her hair. I was amazed by her courage. The wrinkles around his eyes had disappeared and his face again was full of one long bone.

"Come closer, lion," she purred to his fallen mouth. To the jag marks of ancient thrashings below his eyes and the black-lined pink moisture of his nose and the crop of blond, thick hair that bushed outward from his chin.

"Now you've got *so* close—come closer."

The old man paused as though hypnotized. Uncertain. Staring at her face. I suppose at her rain-dark eyes. Drawing down with his great black shag of mane falling close about them both. As he stood there smelling her, I noted, at his height, the maul of this lion would come at the base of the chest without his lifting his jaw.

"I know you won't hunt me," she breathed into his breath. "No you won't."

The old man took one final step and stood over her. She never flinched. He brought his own chest almost to her face and leaned his head out over her. If anything, she lifted her shoulders toward him.

"No, no you won't—" she purred.

And as Molly sat huddled inside the cave of him, it sounded for those few seconds as though the black middle of this lion were humming. The old man swung his head and glared at me then, his good eye ripened to what I could only understand as a challenge. It glowed in the dawn some bellowing kind of amber.

Finally, once he'd lowered his nose and smelled her hair beneath him, actually touching his thick muzzle to her skull, he walked over Molly like a slowly toppling suspension bridge and shambled off into the veld.

•

For the nights thereafter, until our water was nearly gone, and we were rationing severely the cannellini beans that remained, and I was alternately pleading and growing angry then threatening her, Molly acted more than ever as though our camp at Bape, if it were something she hoped to return from at all, was to last as long as the lion. For parts of each night, after the morning he had stood over her, the old man slept beside the truck. In the darkness, through the mesh of the tent, I watched him, his head often set in profile against the ghostly white of the vehicle. Throughout this stretch of nights, he was silent. He never once sighed or huffed as male lions do or gave his low moaning call. In the mornings we'd come out and, by the end, he would frequently remain lying by the truck. If he moved at all, he performed his decrepit ritual of rising one bone at a time and carried his skeleton off to a solitary fever tree where he lay beneath its knobby thorns.

After another week, there were white blooms on that tree because the rains had begun, and Molly and I would sit in the hutch of our puzzle bush behind our collecting canisters for rainwater and look out toward the old man. We no longer drove, seeking the lionesses or the young male. We felt the boom of the wind before the afternoon rains came in, and we would grow hungry watching the distant hustle of honey badgers rooting for dung beetle larvae along the ridge we had once explored. Throughout this period, against my urging, Molly returned most of her rations to the can. She began to lie out flat in the heat and close her eyes. She told me she had been staring into the distance at the wind in the dry scarce trees for those endless days before the rains because she had never prayed before. And that now she wasn't praying only for the lion, but sometimes, when she weakened, as the deep nights came on and her hunger grew fierce, for it all to be over, for hyenas to come with their stoned green eyes.

During these nights, I'd hear the stalling mournful wails of the jackals while I stared out of the tent at the heavy-headed profile of the old man sitting by the truck. Then, at some point during the dark hours, he would let his skull fall soundlessly against the rear tire. Molly, if she slept at all, would awaken in convulsive moments, and reach for me, groping around as if I might soon wander off or already was slipping away. When I held her body close against mine, her skin was moon cold and she was long and deathly light in my arms. Tall grass.

The mineral pans, meanwhile, were quickly softening around us and the mud, even in camp, was steadily deepening. If we failed to start the long trip soon, there was the increasing danger the rains could prevent us from departing at all. As it was, I knew, the way out would be brutal, the plateau already deep in soft mud and standing water, with broad silt lakes and quagmires awaiting us. We had squandered our best chances weeks before and I had allowed the threat of the truck's foundering to grow with each day. Yet Molly informed me each morning, her eyes round and black, that if I left, I'd leave alone.

"We're certainly not helping by staying," I'd protest. "We're likely *hurting* his chances." Or "It's childish to be consumed by the life of one animal." Finally, I'd try, "Why in hell wait for some lion to die?"

All this time, of course, I knew, among other things, the old man was using us for protection. I never once mentioned this to Molly but there was a blood tide of guilt in me. So when I drove out of camp to check conditions on the dirt track north, it was with a strong feeling of my own stupidity and of a more general futility and moroseness. Molly had asked what she never had before, that I leave her for a few hours so she could be alone. I, in the meantime, had been debating whether I should attempt to load her into the truck by force and somehow transport her out against her wishes. I parked the vehicle after just over a mile so the motor would drone off and began my daily search for half-rotten tsamma melons before tracking back to the honey badger's ridge to watch camp. There was a Kalahari apple leaf tree, tall and broad for such loose sand, perched on the ridge. After the rains, it would play host to small white worms which, I knew from my mother, had been a favorite diet of the San. After a time, once I'd stretched out beneath it, I watched Molly rise from the thorny patch beneath our puzzle bush and set out walking toward the old man.

He was some distance away. His twisted fever tree, in bloom from the rains, was like all dryland trees I had been holding in my mind for years. White with its silver hairs sleek and glowing at this early hour of the sun in a kind of soft desert fire.

Molly knelt down before it and faced the lion, whose dark mane I could only dimly make out at that distance. He edged away from her but did not rise.

After a while, which seemed very long to me, she collapsed down all the way. There was no clear movement for a longer time. Then she was up walking back to camp unsteadily, clutching at her face and hair and from time to time doubling over as though to retch, then pulling at low branches of puzzle bush and gathering more from the thorn thatch farther up the hill, so I was forced to shift down into the cover of the grass. She moved back out to the old man and I watched her build a brush wall around him, stretching in a broad circumference around the fever tree. After an hour and a half, it was nearly three feet tall, and I imagined her hands would be bloody and sore. But she didn't stop. She staggered back and forth across the reddish sand, bent over at times, and pausing to rest.

Finally, I walked back along the dirt track to the truck, turned it around, and drove back to camp. Molly was asleep inside the tent, or seemed to be asleep, apparently waiting for the afternoon rains. I looked out toward the fever tree where everything was still. I was shocked, I realized, she had known it somehow to be the time and I had not.

•

The next morning, after we had packed up, which was early, as we'd few things beyond our tent to disassemble, I sat in the truck and waited.

"Come out with me?" she asked. "By now he may be dead."

"I think I'll stay put."

"Please, Jake, just quickly."

I turned the ignition and the truck engine labored and caught.

"I guess not. It's your own damned lion. Anyway—you've walled me out now with the hyenas."

When a few minutes later we walked out to that strangled fever tree together, the thorn brake Molly had built seemed far too thin but quite high, taller than a male Kalahari lion, and it was butchered on one side, away from camp.

Molly gasped. There was no lion inside.

"It's all right, baby," I told her. "C'mon, let's go."

"Were there hyenas?" she asked.

"Could have been. Honestly, I'd rather not know. Now let's head out."

She turned to glare at me straight in the face. "He was definitely still breathing—and I heard nothing last night."

"Would have been lions then. Or must be four or five hyenas. They'll both make big spoor. Hyenas bigger than leopard. Whatever it was would be getting distance from camp."

Molly said nothing, closing her eyes.

"And pug marks," I went on, reluctantly surveying the ground. "Hyena would show blunt claws at the ends of the toes. So it's lion."

She opened her eyes and blinked and stared up at the graying clouds.

"I could walk out and confirm numbers. One's doubled back

here, but no drag marks. Looks like he was still up. Do you want a final count of animals?"

I waited. I had been talking fast. I hadn't looked beyond a first perimeter for scuffle signs or the long soil and turf abrasions that were signals of death because the truth was I didn't want to see.

"Would that matter?" I kept on. I could feel the anger and resentment growing. From where I couldn't say. But they were tall, spiraling masses.

Molly shook her head, held tight between her shoulders, and wept, muttering things I couldn't make out as we walked back to the truck. She began to wail as we drove out of camp. I'd never heard that exact sound before. In fact, I didn't think I could witness such basic grief and take it in. I certainly didn't know, couldn't manage to picture for myself, what it was that was flowing through her. Then, without warning, my own shoulders started to heave at the wheel. I can't cry at all, even poorly. I cannot recall ever weeping in my adult life. But the sound of this was hurting me. Her tears, which I had never seen like this, were flowing, and sinking onto her lap. She was holding herself, hugging herself tightly at heart height. I looked over at her as I drove through the deep red mud, my tires already slipping, locking up and unlocking, the old man gone, and I was sure I hadn't seen or heard anything like this before. Not in her for certain, but not in anyone.

•

After nearly a mile, I halted the truck suddenly. Molly by that point had crumpled in on herself. She was rocking in a ball wedged between the seat and the dash, cramming in her knees with her small head buried and the long, thick black hair matted tightly against her back. She sent out a low moaning sound that filled the vehicle and poured out into the bush.

I waited before I touched her. I stared out the window for a long time in disbelief and confusion. Then in what I guess you could only call awe.

The old man lay sprawled out not thirty feet from the dirt track. Over near a bore hole that ranchers of old or federal wildlife personnel had dug twenty or more years back. There was an old pump there, dilapidated, rusted over, and the handle lay in a jangle of scarred metal on the edge of a depression.

He had what may have been a stolen leopard kill. I can't say. It must have been a good-sized steenbok judging by the length of the vertebral column still largely covered with tawny hide and blood. While I stared, he rose and stood over the carcass for a moment, belly coming round and comical off the clothesline of his spine. He stretched and limped out onto the track so the belly swayed back and forth like a jug of water, grazing one set of legs then the other. Then he bent his good right foreleg to lap at a puddle gathered in the old truck spoor. He wore fresh wounds on his shoulder and face, as though he had come through a high thorn brake to fight something off. I realized just then that all along I had underestimated him terribly, that he was one of those animals who still survived in the Kalahari, who could suffer, endure enormous pain, but would not go down.

Thick clouds were scudding on the plateau. Deep sloughs of red mud dotted the lowlands, and our tires sunk into the sand loam. It had started to rain. I'll admit, in those moments, I thought of driving on. Out of a kind of revenge. To keep everything for myself.

By the time I finally leaned over to touch Molly, the old man had returned to his carcass and began again to feed, his wide paws splayed out and resting on the animal as though it were still alive. I did it slowly, like I was arriving from a far place, from the honey badger's ridge I'd lain on, and through a length of time that included New York somehow, and the mill, and my early life with my parents in the northern Cape, even the long riffs of bush lore I hadn't quite forgotten. I stared at her, still holding back, as though this lion was now all there was of the Africa I had known and the one thing I had left in my life to share.

And it was just in the instant when I said her name aloud—even before she came up black-staring at the old man and swallowing air, gasping then flashing out her arms so one clocked me in the head, before any of it—that I knew a wild life and a thousand years shaking down the dirt track.

"Molly," I said quietly—"Molly."

WILDERNESS

Throughout the winter in the wake of her father's death, Kathy worked sprawled on her bedroom floor and wrapped herself in blankets and scarcely left the apartment. She thought his death might brush past her silently, so he would be gone. But during those long snow months, his voice, even the eyes, stayed alive, winter-starved. They trailed her when she entered her deep closet or slipped through the narrow door from one room to the other.

She'd majored in engineering in college and now she made maps, as an illustrator and cartographic designer. After working for the Park Service in an office job in Sacramento and then for a local commission tracking precipitation levels along elevation gradients west of Reno, she'd moved back east to Boston and toiled mainly on her laptop. Though, now and then, a specialty client solicited hand-drawn maps and she would sketch the round faces of winds or the silken garments of an alluvial river at flood. From the outset, her mapping came with fieldwork and brought her to overland navigation in forests, in mountains, and in deserts. So in the summers for extra funds, she taught wayfinding courses, weeklong or three-day intensive, and helped clients use land features and vertical relief for orientation purposes in wilderness contexts. But in winters, or late autumns, or early springs, she went out to these places alone, not for work.

There were men who occasionally came with her on these trips, and some of them she'd loved, sparingly, with the part of her that wasn't taken already by the lure of something wild. "But for what?" they would ask. "You're looking for what?" and sometimes, beside a night fire or inside the tent or on a rock face where she was strung to a man by rope, she would try to explain. "It's the feeling when you're out alone—then you push so far you can't believe it's happening." And when they said nothing to this, she would go on, more for herself: "But it is."

Now, soon after the snows, after the presence of her father's voice, his eyes, had waned to the pitch, the shade, of a haunting, she loaded her gear and drove north to the Adirondack Mountains in upstate New York. Her parents had owned a place on a deep glacial lake within the boundary of the national park for decades, but in the last months of her father's life they'd sold it. While it was a financial necessity to sell, Kathy mourned the place. She would plunge into the lake and dive down beside the smooth granite walls of the shoreline into the gloom. Her father would lean out from the rocks to watch. Suspended at depth, she could hear the throb of her pulse and, looking upward, see splotches for his shoulders migrate in the oil of her vision. She would wait far down until her chest was revving. Then rise through cold green water toward the wavering moon of his face.

When Kathy arrived at the cabin she'd rented she saw with relief it was far from the road beside a shallow brook as the owner had advertised. It was a hundred miles from the lake house in a part of the forest she hadn't explored. Here, twilight gilded the tops of blue-eyed grass surrounding a stand of balsam fir. The firs loomed tall and rickety over the ironed current of the brook in these stretched-out moments before dark. All of it smelled like water, but water in motion, of minerals mixed with the cold air of the wind rushing above the folded rips. And as she approached the banks the air grew colder, rising from the dark flow to sweep over her body, until she entered another atmosphere.

•

Her father had taken exception to her activities in the outdoors. He'd judged them, rightly she'd always believed, to involve risk. What's more, he'd found the risks she took tramping through deep forest, or on glaciated terrain both domestically and abroad, or in slot canyons and desert landscapes where she stayed out weeks at a time, to be unacceptably high. Again and again, he would come back to her size and sex. She was of medium height but thin and sinewy, too small in his eyes if something were to go wrong. Lacking the strength. And she would freeze to death with such little reserve.

"You're a lightweight," he'd told her. "I've seen your pack. How're you humping supplies so long without breaking down under all that volume?"

When she shrugged and told him she was fit and careful, a planner, that she carried emergency gear in case things went badly, he interrupted, waving his hand.

"What's out there anyway?" he asked. "I mean it. What's there that's not here?"

Now the winter was giving up early in the Adirondacks. Inside the rental cabin Kathy covered herself in blankets, enough to stop shivering, until her body in that cocoon grew warm and light. She slept late, far into the morning. Peering out from her bed she could see slabs of ice trail over the remains of a beaver dam and catch there, chunked and suspended. Her ears were still full of the highway and of her father saying she was getting too old to be so alone. She needed to marry at last, come up from her depths, before it was too late. "Must be someone," he'd ventured shyly, "to scoop up a thin, long-haired girl like you."

It was almost five years since the last time he said those things. Now she was thirty-seven. Even so, she could hear his stricken voice as if it rode an old, trailing wind. Or were breath of the black earth.

•

By midafternoon, the brook was flecked with silt when she knelt to sink her arm to the shoulder in the icy slurry. She left it there until the first electric jags of pain shot down from her elbow into her wrist. Here was the familiar feeling of deep cold, of water surrounding her skin and the long bones inside, touching through to the blood.

Already, fog hovered low to the ground. The weather was changing. There had been stars the night before. Orion's bright sword at his belt. Now the visibility would be poor. Darkness would come earlier than on another night in this season. So she decided not to wait. She changed and locked the cabin and set out into thick forest to the west.

The going was a mix of ice, still bulked, and seasonal water spilt into hollows. Kathy toiled through peeling birch stands that had seen little rain. Brittle now so early in the season. In the tree wells, all of the snow was cached. But on the higher pitches where the canopy thinned, only a crisp membrane of winter remained on the ground. As she headed uphill, she left her old magnetic compass, cracked at the bezel, in her pack, watching the placement of lichen on trees, tracking swatches of brightness against the sky to confirm her bearings. But there was no sunset. And in this swamp of wet air, the fog became a spectral carrier of light.

She was warm and removed her light shell and tied it to her waist. Then allowed herself to think of wolves. They would be hungry with the thaw. And active in this new warmth before the period of their denning. Having read online that a resident winter pack presided over fifteen square miles while hunting farther afield, she'd mapped the timing and locations of area sightings. She'd illustrated her topographical rendering with the outlines of wolves and a ranging, sinuous sketch of herself: mostly thick, black hair stretched through the woods, until she was tangled into the trees.

Kathy removed her long-sleeved flannel shirt and reshouldered her pack. She walked in her tank top and allowed the warm, damp shirt to trail behind her, dangling from her fingers. After a short time, she let it drop to the leaf litter. As she picked her way forward it grew fully dark, then less so, glowing faintly in places in the woods. The fog was lifting, the waning moon still above a quarter. Now a low shifting breeze channeled through the trees so she walked in and out of the cold as through soft currents in the woods at night.

Skirting a wide beaver pond, she scanned the close horizon. There would be devastation, with trees gnawed down and half-skinned for their bark. But all she could glimpse was the faint gleam of water morphing to darkness as it spread beyond her vision. Kathy pulled off her tank top and laid it atop the deep melt layer. It floated wanly in the afterlight before wilting down. As she walked off, her skin was cool and damp where the fabric had been. The shoulder harness of her pack had collected moisture and rested now on her sports bra and bare skin. So the wet straps lay close enough to her neck to awaken her heartbeat and tap the wellsprings of her blood.

•

Once she'd left the swamp and passed into stinging bracken, a shape came across her path, then another. And she froze. Kathy had never met wolves in the wild. As she watched, the forms materialized, grew firm, and dissolved. Then they were off to her right, at a greater distance. There was almost no sound attached to their movements. There was almost no movement. Only the trading out of places in the brush. Possibly whitetails, Kathy thought. A dispersed female group. Knowing instinctively, they were not deer. Or coyote. Too large by far for fisher or fox. And they were in numbers. But the truth was she had seen next to nothing. If she'd seen less, any less, they would not have been there at all. In any case, whatever was out there, in motion around her, it was not deer.

The moon made a faint presence. She never saw it beyond a gradual saturation, a glow in the cloud cover. The fog had lifted then returned and lifted again. Now she opened her pack and ate the lunch that had slipped past dinner to a midnight repast, then almost slipped past that. She was eating, she decided, just in time, to center the night. To keep it from passing in one fell shadow. As if all winter long, since news of her father's death, she'd flown beneath a goshawk, sunk within the shade of its wings.

Afterward, she turned to the north and headed into country she hadn't studied on the topographical map or included in her own drawing of local contour lines wherein, beside those dark skeins of her hair gathered into forest, the long sketch of her body curved to join rivers.

Now, without a line of sight on the ridgelines and in the absence of stars, she couldn't be sure of her bearings. But she felt it was north, as if the needle inside her had been wavering for slow, sad months, an entire snow season, and only here, at night, with the appearance of animals, did it steel to its heading.

Having so recently seen them around her and noted their direction of travel, Kathy arched her spine and tilted her shoulders down and back. She brought her lean arms tightly behind her and let her hands dangle for a moment. She waited, listening. Then she eased her pack to the ground with a flask of water, her compass and med kit, a space blanket inside, and moved off toward the sounds through tight, smudged trees.

•

Her father had claimed he was the only one who could shake her from her inwardness. From hell-bent stupidity. He'd gone on about how she should heed his warnings. She must harken to his voice even when somewhere far off. She'd reminded him she was trained after all, with experience in remote terrain. But he shrugged this off. Then turned to insults or prepared speeches. When none of it worked, the visits to her parents' house in New Hampshire became strained and often silent. He would ignore her completely or praise everyone else or grow furious and mumble so she could barely understand.

"But why are you doing this?" she'd asked finally, cornering him in the narrow kitchen.

She'd managed to surprise him with her question and, after that first instant, his face sloughed anger to reveal something open, like a plea, with the eyes bluing out. "I'd like to take you with me," she thought of saying. But she didn't say anything that was real. That she actually felt.

He looked at her, searching, she could tell, in just the way she was searching for him. Like probe lights from a ravaged city had entered the room then paused over their faces, even come back. But found nothing. Anyway, he was gone. She'd survived him. He was cold in his grave, poor man. She couldn't worry him now. She was beyond his worry.

Now Kathy crashed into leafless winter branches that left deep scratches on her face and arms and across her bare shoulders. Nettles, recently denuded of ice, brought welts with long, raised contours over her ribs that stung to the touch and dampened her fingers. In pursuit of whatever it was she'd seen, she sought traces of motion against the darkness. The moon had set and she was deep in the lowlands, between escarpments, among larch and alder. Here, in the spruce flats, she trundled through witch hobble. And bumped against white pine. The ground had a crunch layer she broke through in crisp rhythm. Her heart meanwhile grew fierce in her chest as if it were calling out to the low damp woods.

She halted and removed her boots. She had matches in the right pocket of her pants and a fixed, sawback blade sheathed at her belt, where they always were. She undid the frayed woolen pants she could wear wet and had worn in many, many places over the years. She'd joked with someone they were more valuable than skin. That inside them she could survive both fire and flood. Now she let them drop to the leaves and stepped out of the cuffs, sliding her boots on again. She undid the knotted arms of her shell that hung about her waist and curled them loosely around one wrist so the first slow tendrils of heat stole into her flesh and began to gather there. But before this low warmth could take hold, she shook her wrist free.

"Now I'm a woman walking in my boots," she whispered out into the trees.

Kathy pushed on toward highlands she sensed in her ankles and by the fact that her toes, in rising country, knew the ground better than her heels. Straining, she worked through the thick duff of hemlock. When she crossed a narrow brook, the current of air stiffened her thighs and rocked chill into her knees. At last, on reaching a low saddle where the ground fell steeply ahead and climbed at her sides, she found no more light but felt presences. Out into the distance, when the new day broke, would stretch a vision of trees. A vast, slanted forest of spruce and white pine pitching down into the valley. No doubt with state roads intersecting. She must be nearing roads. There was a feeling, in that same instant, of movement nearby. Then the slow-weighted crackle of ice and leaves.

•

Due to her job, but more because of her love for it, she'd been often out of doors since her early twenties, gradually amassing experience not only with rugged conditions, storm events, and client mishaps, but with wildlife. Kathy thrilled to these encounters with other animals. They were dark steps into the unknown, where you could give something out and get back what wasn't available elsewhere in the world. Then, despite the risk, or because of it, see beyond yourself. But from the beginning her father looked at them askance. He'd been a corporate lawyer. A problem solver. He broke things down and saw two sides, pitted against one another.

“For now, it’s white-tailed deer. So course you get the coyotes.”

He’d grown very sick. It was in his last years. There was no more following him through rooms or cornering him somewhere. She stood beside his bed.

He motioned for her to sit close because his voice, turned gravelly in the months before, was down to a grated whisper. Even so, he looked at the ceiling while he talked as if to lose track of her eyes. His chest was shrunk in. And the arms, just drifting bones under loose, creped skin, were pasted to his sides.

“Fact is, moose are coming down to northern New York from Algonquin. Breeding successfully through the wetlands. So there’s all those new calves.”

He spoke slowly enough she wondered how he would finish. How he’d hold on to his will, or the fear, in the midst of this decay. When his face turned toward her, it looked borrowed, sallow, and unreadable. But for some reason, that was the face she could remember.

“And with them come your wolves.”

Kathy changed course now away from the sounds. She headed for dry uplands. If there was exposed rock, an isolated crag, she might extend her line of sight and clamber out of reach if she had to. At least gain the advantage of high ground. As the trees were too weak to climb—red spruce, stands of stunted beech—she stooped for felled branches and chose one heavy enough to wield. Again, she was sweating, but only scarcely now. Her throat was raw, and the night’s intermittent cold left her wrists weak and fingers lame, tingling when she worked them, then slowly numbing out.

At the top, she found a haggard summit but no crag. She flushed a bird of some kind, sizable by the rough noise of its flight. At any moment the sun, still climbing beneath the rim of the horizon, would presage itself. Kathy imagined, whatever they were, they might circle the brow of the hill and come in from behind. In all likelihood there would be a second col in that direction, deeper than the one she'd reached. If they were wolves, they would use the land to remain hidden, then come in gliding from both sides at once.

After dense silence, she noted a faint profile, first one then several, up to five, at some remove from each other and in motion. Their winter shag was lighter than the color of the diminished night, the faces lighter still, the close-set eyes nearly yellow, living in instants, in a kind of shimmer, when the heads, dim triangles, turned toward her against the movement of the bodies. They were unmistakable, tall, brushing the limbs of sparse trees. And they worked together with what remained of the night, moving slowly through gaps of suddenness.

Kathy widened her stance and raised the heavy branch until it was even with her shoulders. Until it would come even with their risen heads. But she didn't swing it or menace the air. Or cry out in an attempt at intimidation. Nor did she inhale deeply to expand her rib cage or bare her teeth or raise a fist to stretch her torso and make herself appear larger, more imposing. She'd used such strategies when encountering predators before. But now she shrunk herself down.

•

There were things her father said in the last two years that left his barrages and silences behind. There had been, she decided, depending on how you looked at it, a kind of détente. As she stood in his dark room and stared out the windows beyond the sprawling canopy bed, he came back to what he'd read about wolves as if to seek her out before he was gone.

"They can scent your blood past a mile off," he told her softly. "And they're smarter than us. They know you're armed by the smell of your confidence. How you hold your body. And they won't just listen to voices—they'll watch your hands. What you're wearing. What you're hiding under all those layers. They'll notice your pack." He sighed deeply. "It's not just checking for weapons, see? They're looking for weakness."

With long distances between his sentences, as if traveling through spaces where he was no longer alive, her father explained that wolves rarely attack without the stimulus of pursuit. They wait for their prey—even a musk ox that will stand its ground then pivot in deep snow—to tremble and run. To give in to its fears. With a chase underway, there are short barks before they move to the jugular or groin to tap the blood. Until then, timber wolves often linger, closing with a slow, deliberate weighting of their shoulders, prompting the animal to betray itself.

"Sure, okay, but I'm not afraid of wolves, all right? Since we've shot and trapped them to hell for cash or revenge, or just sport, doubt they'd stick around to make a still target. Being smart as you say."

Kathy breathed quietly in his presence, unsure of herself. The feeling it was almost over, that he would be gone, made her want to speak also, to save him.

"To get hunted like you're talking now, you know, I'd have to work hard. Truth is—" She couldn't look at him. His whole face was unbearably open and attentive, full of yearning. "I'm more a danger to myself."

His skin was jaundiced. Yet with a sheen. She'd never admitted that to anyone before. He was a radiant presence, in the lock of pain.

"But wolves, no. I'd have to get weak, real vulnerable. Even then—honestly, bet you can let that go."

In strange slow motion, the lines on his brow pulled taut. His mouth stretched wide in a still-frame of agony. There was so little flesh anyway, just the shape of his skull.

"Now there's your problem—we're hardwired to flee those animals. Not scared of them, you're not scared of anything."

"No, no," she interrupted. "Wait, not true—I am afraid."

"Of what then?"

For once the question came fast but she didn't answer. Despite the fact he'd given her his eyes. That he wanted to know, she was sure of it. He'd left the muskeg and alder thickets, or wherever he'd been. He was looking into her, allowing her this chance.

But Kathy stood before him mute, staring at his wasted body.

"Anyone should be afraid in your chosen position," he breathed. "They'll eat organs out first. Of your caribou, your moose, even beaver. Then move on to muscle tissue."

•

A cold sun limned the horizon before it was even a sun. And when she grew tired in her crouch and her legs became candles, quivering, burning down into her feet, she loosened her grip and let the branch fall from her hands.

She lay down to wait on the broad plinth of the summit at the base of two wind-broken boles of spruce. She lay there balled, hunching in her shoulders. Then stretched out fully and brought her arms tightly to her sides. She decided this was what it must be for her father. Without warmth. Or the windmill of the blood. Lacking speech and breath. And no water inside. She sang a thin snatch of hymn that hung above her and disappeared down into the valley.

Then, after a delay, came the low, answering huff of animals from the broken timber. Fumbling, she removed her boots. Clumsy and nearly frozen, she shimmied out of her sports bra and underwear. She was naked in this wan light, wearing the bright print of trees.

Over time when she'd been still the wolves closed in to wind her deeply, taking shape as a singleton then in groups of two or three. They fanned out and showed their winter shoulders, slim as blades. Their flanks were narrow after long months since moose and white-tail ruts had gathered prey in the barrels of valleys. Now, before the birthing season would leave calves and does newly vulnerable, the pack was famished, emboldened. The bodies were elongated from the side and slanted down the spine from the dark neck patch toward the tail. And in brief snatches she could smell them. It was the old, still smell of rusted coils and algal ponds.

One came forward. Young, scenting her, setting then weighting each paw. There was no threat display or obvious aggression. He drew closer along an arc with his steep-set muzzle and close augur's eyes angled toward her. Hugging in her knees, she stared back and waited for him to bristle. To bring up his ears from the thick ruff. Level his plush, black-tipped tail. But he did none of these things. So when he reached a point six meters off, she spoke in a way she didn't speak to humans.

"Okay, come close," she whispered. "But I won't move."

At the sound of her voice, he hackled. His face pinched and recoiled. He suspended his breath to listen, hitching his jaw. There was a light tick to that change. His shoulders squared off and dipped nearly to the ground. Sleeked out, he inched forward so she shifted her body in the dirt to face him dead-on. Until they were locked to each other. Then when she could make out the pale swatches of fur between his eyes and the moisture of the nostrils and their brief, rapid expansions, she brought her hands from her armpits for him to see them empty and laid them open against her knees.

Through the night, she'd dwelled on the red Algonquin wolf, the eastern gray, how they were carrying deep memories now too. She'd come back to her father winter-ghosting. Rumbling about her rooms. There were the cracked speeches urging caution when his shot voice rose high and light. Then his staring and waiting.

But that call, those eyes, were losing ground. "Please," she'd gasped in deep bottomlands while she sought the sound of animals. "This is what I was afraid of. Don't you know?"

Now the wolf drifted sideways, as in a place of water. He planted and retracted a paw. When he held it briefly aloft, her body grew down and rooted in the mountain. The sun sipped the steeping sky. Then her cold, dark hair, run over her shoulders and hung past her ribs and pooled on her raw, cold feet, became the thing she had on.

"Come."

NIGHTS FROM THIS GALAXY

Many years ago now, we went to the home of a professor and his wife. His wife did all the talking, while the professor politely listened. When one of us spoke up over capers and sole, he nodded sagely, as if we had dived into the sea and recovered a lost treasure of knowing. There was a view from their windows out over the wide city that shone in isolated sparks of resplendent light which never came together. Throughout, I had the feeling we would remember that night long after he was gone.

While his wife described her work, he rose often and refilled our glasses. He trundled with our dishes to the sink in the kitchen with a lumbering purity that made him seem both a giant and a feather. Once, toward the end, he mentioned he was in the grip of a book, that he was composing whenever he could. "It was the hardest thing," his lips seemed to say, speaking of his labors. I thought of Sartre, and de Beauvoir, and Hurston, and Neruda, all of the thousand ones who had written in cities. I imagined him at the cramped desk beside the table, his papers piled up before him. He was sure, he said, one day he would finish. And when he answered my wife's questions, when he fielded her curiosity, he smiled and agreed with her, though he was the writer of the book. The way he was, he could transfer to you, or to anyone, the fruits of his toil, as though you had divined them from an open hand, found someone's fortune in lines on a palm, and now were only retailing those lineaments, the faintest, limned features, that scarcely betokened the depth of your long fathoming.

Finally, the meal was over. We rose to leave. I thanked him, and it was my one time with him, just before he turned to my wife, when I felt the warmth of his eyes. For a moment, there was a pause, or maybe I paused and so he was forced to do the same. Then he was sending his plaudits to both of us, affording the most earnest assurances of his belief in the resilience, the hardihood of our world. For a long time, the seconds poured out, though we were only walking toward the door. There was the quiet music of the loud city, many floors down. And the knowledge we were still present, on the threshold.

We held hands, walking through the splayed lights of the city, all the way home. And since then, he has died, and nights are warm, and our earth is changing, holding in the ruin we bestow. The evenings we have together are lovely, but they are ominous. The animals around us are dying. Landscapes bear their last, soundless steps like museums. Now, I believe, we are all writing in cities, of one form or another. Once, I looked into the matter of whether the professor had finished his book in time, before he died. I hoped his words would be tracks in the earth, and deep, inmost life had survived. But, like so many things, I found it nowhere.

ACKNOWLEDGMENTS

I am grateful to the following magazines and anthology where these stories appeared:

"Lion" in *Prairie Schooner* and *The O. Henry Prize Stories*

"Coyote" and "Leviathan" in *Conjunctions*

"Run" in *Raritan*

"One Road" in *Slush Pile Magazine*

"The Canoeist" in *Michigan Quarterly Review*

"Three Parts of Hunger" in *Kenyon Review*

"Wilderness" in *EPOCH*

"Nights From This Galaxy" in *New Letters*

Thank you to Michelle Weitzel, Joanna Starr, Loretta Weitzel, Gretchen Van Der Heyden, Debbie Boeck, and Elizabeth Molle.